FIFTY CANDLES

EARL DERR BIGGERS

FIFTY CANDLES

EARL DERR BIGGERS

Introduction and frontispiece by

JOHN GREGORY BETANCOURT

WILDSIDE PRESS

CONTENTS

INTRODUCTION

JOHN GREGORY BETANCOURT

Earl Derr Biggers (1884-1933) is best remembered as the creator of Chinese detective Charlie Chan, whose long-running series of exploits (portrayed in the movies first by Warner Oland and later Sidney Toler) made him a world-famous character from the 1930s to the 1950s. At the height of the series, Charlie Chan was nearly on par with Sherlock Holmes…and he spawned such Oriental detective imitators as Mr. Moto and Mr. Wong.

Biggers had always been interested in mystery fiction, but his interest in Hawaii clearly stems from a 1919 vacation in Honolulu. While there, he read a newspaper article on a Chinese detective named Chang Apana. Apana would become the model for Charlie Chan in Biggers' 1925 novel, *House Without a Key*, and there quickly followed five more Charlie Chan novels.

Fifty Candles—published just two years after that 1919 vacation—shows how Hawaii, China, and murder had already begun to come together in Biggers' imagination. The story starts in a courthouse in Honolulu, moves to China, then to fog-shrouded San Francisco. Many of the elements used in the Charlie Chan series are present: Chinese characters (both sinister and sympathetic), the Honolulu legal system, a shrewd detective (in this case, the lawyer Mark Drew rather than a policemen), and a baffling murder complete with red herrings and plenty of suspects.

Though *Fifty Candles* is a murder mystery, it is also a romance, with the romantic elements at times in the forefront. Mostly, though, it is a book that will delight Biggers' many fans as they trace the origins of Charlie Chan.

Several other Earl Derr Biggers novels are currently available from Wildside Press, including a murder mystery set in London entitled *The Agony Column*.

FIFTY CANDLES

CHAPTER I

From the records of the district court at Honolulu for the year 1898 you may, if you have patience, unearth the dim beginnings of this story of the fifty candles. It is a story that stretches over twenty years, all the way from that bare Honolulu courtroom to a night of fog and violence in San Francisco. Many months after the night of the tule-fog, I happened into the Hawaiian capital and took down from a library shelf a big legal-looking book, bound in bright yellow leather the color of a Filipino houseboy's shoes on his Saturday night in town. I found what I was looking for under the heading: "In the Matter of Chang See."

The Chinese, we are told, are masters of indirection, of saying one thing and meaning another, of arriving at their goal by way of a devious, irrelevant maze. Our legal system must have been invented and perfected by Chinamen—but is this *lèse majesté* or contempt of court or something? Beyond question the decision of the learned court in the matter of Chang See, as set down in the big yellow book, is obscured and befuddled by a mass of unspeakably dreary words. See 21 Cyc., 317 Church *Habeas Corpus*, 2d Ed., Sec. 169. By all means consult Kelley *v.* Johnson, 31 U. S. (6 Pet.) 622, 631-32. And many more of the same sort.

Here and there, however, you will happen on phrases that mean something to the layman; that indicate, behind the barrier of legal verbiage, the presence of a flesh-and- blood human fighting for his freedom—for his very life. Piece these phrases together and you may be able to reconstruct the scene in the courtroom that day in 1898, when a lean impassive Chinaman of thirty stood alone against the great American nation. In other words, Chang See *v.* U. S.

I say he stood alone, though he was, of course, represented by counsel. "Harry Childs for the Petitioner," says the big yellow book. Poor Harry Childs—his mind was already beginning to go. It had been keen enough when he came to the islands, but the hot sun and the cool drinks—well, he was a little hazy that day in court. He died long ago—just shriveled up and died of an overdose of the Paradise of the Pacific—so it can hardly injure his professional standing to intimate that he was of little aid to his client, Chang See.

Chang See was petitioning the United States for a writ of *habeas corpus* and his freedom from the custody of the inspector of immigration at the port of Honolulu. He had arrived at the port from China some two months previously, bringing with him a birth certificate recently obtained and forwarded to him by friends in Honolulu. This certificate asserted that Chang See had been born in Honolulu of Chinese parents—that he had first seen the light on a December day thirty years before in a house out near Queen Emma's yard, on the beach at Waikiki. When he was four years old his parents had taken him back with them to their native village of Sun Chin, in China.

If the certificate spoke the truth, then Chang See must be regarded as an American citizen and freely admitted to Honolulu with no wearisome chatter about the Chinese Exclusion Act. But the inspector at the port had been made wary by long service. He admitted that the certificate was undoubtedly founded on fact. But, he contended, how was he to know that this tall, wise-looking Chinaman was the little boy Chang See who had once played about the beach at Waikiki?

Thus challenged, the petitioner brought in witnesses to prove his identity. He brought twelve of them in all—shuffling old men, ancient dames with black silk trousers and tiny feet, younger sports prominent in the night life of Hotel Street. Some of them were reputed to have known him as a baby out near Queen Emma's yard; others had been the companions of the days of his youth in the village of Sun Chin.

Chang See's witnesses had begun their testimony before the inspector confidently enough. Then under the inspector's stony stare they had weakened. They had become confused, contradictory. Even the man who had obtained the birth certificate gave as the name of Chang See's father an entirely new and unheard-of appellation. In a word, the petitioner's friends one and all deserted him. Something seemed to have happened to them.

And something *had* happened to them. That something was the vivid remembrance of a little old lady with a thin face and cruel eyes, who was at the moment sitting in Peking, the virtual ruler of all China. Chang See had been lately active in fields that did not appeal to the dowager empress. He had been one of the group of brilliant reformers who had come so near winning the young emperor to their way of thinking, until that day in September when the empress had put down her foot, with its six-inch Manchu sole. She had made the emperor practically a prisoner in the palace and had announced that those who wished to change the existing order in China would please see her first. And if she saw them first—

She didn't see many of them. They fled for their lives, Chang See among them. His witnesses knew this. They knew that the little old lady was sitting waiting in the midst of her web at Peking—waiting and hoping for the return of Chang See. They knew that the dear old thing had virtually promised to have a man ready with a basket to catch Chang See's head as it fell. Overcome with fear for themselves, for their people at home, they became foggy of mind, uncertain of names and dates. And Chang See's case smashed on the rock of their indifference.

It is not surprising, therefore, that the inspector of immigration was not convinced of the petitioner's identity. Following the usual formula, Harry Childs appealed the case to Washington.

The officials there, with unexpected promptness, agreed with the inspector, and Chang See was driven to his last resort. He besought the district court in Honolulu for a writ; and on a certain morning in December, '98—as a matter of fact it must have been Chang See's birthday, provided he *was* Chang See—he stood awaiting the decision of the judge.

I can picture that scene in court for you, partly from the records, partly from the story of one who was there and remembers. Judge Smith was presiding; "H. Smith," he has it in the yellow book, with the modesty required of judges by custom. He was a big, blond, cool-looking man with a rather peevish manner not uncommon among whites in a tropic country. He sat idly thumbing the pages of his decision. There were a good many of them, he noticed. The languid hour of noon was approaching, and through his mind flashed a vision of his *lanai*, close by the white breakers at Waikiki. An armchair and magazines just in from the mainland awaited him there; also bottles, glasses, and ice, all of which were capable of being brought into delightful touch with one another.

H. Smith took a sip from a glass at his elbow—indubitably water—and began to read. He had, he said, studied with great diligence the petition submitted by counsel, which, he added with a disapproving glance at Harry Childs, was unnecessarily long and involved. The petitioner, as he understood it, based his application for a right to land on the assertion that he was Chang See, born of Chinese parents in Honolulu thirty years before, in a house near Queen Emma's yard at Waikiki. If the assertion were true, if the petitioner were Chang See, then as an American citizen he must be granted all he sought. But was this petitioner Chang See? The matter was clouded by grave doubts. Pass over the fact that he had waited more than twenty-nine years before asking for his birth certificate. Pass over as well the fact that the man who had obtained the certificate had later, by his testimony, appeared uncertain of the name of Chang See's father. Turn to the testimony of the petitioner's other witnesses.

He analyzed that testimony. He tore it to shreds. All at once he was reminded of the case *in re* Wang Chi-tung, 3 U. S. District Court, Hawaii 601-610. He was reminded of other anecdotes of a like nature. His voice droned on and on. The clerk of court fumbled sleepily at his watch fob and scowled at Chang See, the petitioner. All this time wasted!

H. Smith grew more genial when he came to the final page of his decision. After all, it had not taken so long as he expected. Summing it all up, quoting a few more authorities, he admitted at last that he shared the doubts of the inspector and the officials at Washington. He therefore, he added quite pleasantly, remanded the petitioner into the custody of the Inspector of Immigration for deportation to China.

The petitioner was a student who understood many languages, and he needed no interpreter to translate for him the words of the judge. He heard them, however, without so much as the flicker of an eyelash. We know now that he was Chang See. There was no justice in the world for him that day; but no one could have read his despair in his face. Harry Childs, on the other hand, was not a nerveless Oriental. His tobacco heart ablaze with anger, the lawyer leaped to his feet and did a most unprofessional thing.

"With all due respect to the dignity of this court," he cried, "I wish to advise Your Honor that you have sentenced this man to his death. Owing to his activities for reform in China, there is a price on his head there today. I wish to add—I wish to say—" He faltered under the angry glare bent upon him by H. Smith. "I wish to repeat and emphasize—you have sentenced this man to his death!"

Harry Childs had never been in high favor in that court, and if looks could kill he would then and there have preceded his client into eternity. Outwardly, however, the judicial calm was unruffled.

"The matter brought up by the learned counsel," said the judge—and legal verbiage sometimes lends itself admirably to sarcasm—"is not one involved in the petition as presented. I need hardly add that I regard it as a matter with which this court has no concern. The court is adjourned."

Chang See stood waiting not far from the judge's bench. Into his eyes had come an expression of amused contempt which might have annoyed the learned judge had he seen it. But H. Smith was already on his way to the cottage at Waikiki. He waited, did the Chinaman, until the inspector came for him, and they started down the aisle together. It was only a narrow path between the benches, but it was the beginning of the road that must lead Chang See back to China and a most unpleasant death. Yet he set out on it with his head held high and with a firm brave step.

Did Chang See tread that path to its logical and bitter end? Did he come in time to the edge of the web in the center of which the dowager empress, spiderlike, sat waiting? The story, as has been said, stretches over twenty years, and the succeeding chapters may seem, at first glance, irrelevant. But before we finish we shall be able to put together the pieces of our Chinese puzzle and know the end of the path that led at first between two rows of benches in a Honolulu court.

CHAPTER II

Twenty years later, toward the close of 1918, I stepped from the gangplank of a China boat and for the first time in my life set foot in San Francisco. If you have always thought of San Francisco as the bonny merry city, the gay light-hearted city, I advise you not to enter it first when it is wrapped in the gloom of fog. You will suffer a sad disappointment, such as I knew on landing that dark December afternoon.

Heaven knows I ought to have been a happy man that day, fog or no fog, for I was coming back to my own land after four dreary years in China. Birds should have been singing, as the Chinese say, is the topmost branches of my heart; I should have walked with a brisk, elated tread. Instead I crossed the dimly lighted pier shed, where yellow lamps burned wanly overhead, with lagging step, dragging my battered old bags after me. The injustice of the world lay heavy on my heart. For I was young, and I had been unfairly treated. Four years earlier, just graduated from the engineering department of a big technical institution in the East, I had set sail from Vancouver to take charge of a mine in China for Henry Drew. In Shanghai I met the old San Francisco millionaire , a little yellow-faced man with snapping black eyes and long thin hands that must have begun, even in the cradle, to reach and seize and hold.

The mine, he told me frankly, was little better than a joke so far. Its future was up to me. I would encounter many obstacles—inadequate pumping machinery, bribe-hunting officials, superstitious workmen fearful of disturbing the earth dragon as our shaft sank deeper. If I could conquer in spite of everything, accomplish a miracle, and make the mine pay, then in addition to my salary I was to receive a third interest in the property. I suppose he really meant it at the time. He said it more than once. I was very young, with boundless faith. I did not get that part of it in writing.

Through four awful years I labored for Henry Drew down there in Yunnan, the province of the cloudy south. One by one the obstacles gave way and copper began to come from the mine. Now and then ugly disquieting rumors as to the sense of honor of old Drew drifted to me, but I put them resolutely out of my thoughts.

I might seem guilty of boasting if I went into details regarding the results of my work. It is enough to say that I succeeded. Again I met Henry Drew in Shanghai, and he told me he was proud of me. I ventured to remind him of his promise of an interest in the property. He said I must be dreaming. He recalled no such promise. I was appalled. Could such things be? Angrily and at length I told him what I thought of him. He listened in silence.

"I'll accept it," he said when I paused for breath.

"Accept what?" I asked.

"Your resignation."

He got it, along with further comments on his character. I went back to my hotel to take up the difficult task of securing accommodations on a homebound boat.

All liners were crowded to suffocation in those days, but I finally managed to get a November sailing. I was informed that I, along with another male passenger, would be put into the cabin of the ship's doctor. Rumor had told me that old Henry Drew was sailing on the same boat, but I was hardly prepared, when I went on board and entered my stateroom, to find him bending over an open bag. Fate in playful mood had selected him as the third member of our party.

He was more upset than I and made a strenuous effort to be assigned to some other room. But with all his money he could not manage it, and we set out on our homeward journey together. I would see him when I came in late at night, lying there in his berth with the light from the deck outside on his yellow face, his eyes closed—but wide awake. I think he was afraid of me. He had reason to be.

Anyhow, I was rid of his slimy presence now, there in that dim pier shed. It was one thing to be thankful for. And already the memory of what he had done to me was fading—for I had suffered a later and deeper wound. In the midst of the trouble with Drew, I had met the most wonderful girl in the world, and only a moment before, on the deck of the China boat, I had said good-bye to her forever.

I left the pier shed and stepped to the sidewalk outside. The air was heavy and wet with fog, the walk damp and slippery; water dripped down from telegraph wires overhead. I saw the blurred lights of the city, heard its ceaseless grumble, the clang of street-cars, the clatter of wheels on cobblestones. Weird mysterious figures slipped by me; strange faces peered into mine and were gone. This was the Embarcadero, the old Barbary Coast famed round the world. Somewhere there, lost in the fog, were its dance-halls, where rovers of the broad Pacific had, in the vanished past, made merry after a sodden fashion. I stood, straining to see.

"Want a taxi, mister?" asked a dim figure at my side.

"If you can find one," I answered. "Things seem a bit thick."

"It's the tule-fog," he told me. "Drifts down every year about this time from the tule-fields between here and Sacramento. Never knew one to stick around so late in the day before. Yes, sir—this is sure unusual."

In reply to my query he told me that the tule was a sort of bulrush. And little Moses amid his bulrushes could have felt no more lost than I did at that moment.

"See what you can dig up," I ordered.

"You just wait here," he said. "It'll take time. Don't go away."

Again I stood alone amid the strange shadow-shapes that came and went. Somewhere, behind that fog-curtain, the business of the town went on as usual. I made a neat pile of my luggage close to a telegraph pole and sat down to wait. My mind went back to the deck of the boat I had left, to Mary Will Tellfair, that wonderful girl.

And she was wonderful—in courage and in charm. I had met her three weeks before in Shanghai; and it was her dark hour, as it was mine. For Mary Will had come five thousand miles to marry Jack Paige, her sweetheart from a sleepy southern town. She had not seen him for six years, but there had been many letters, and life at home was dull. Then, too, she had been very fond of him once, I judge. So there had been parties, and jokes, and tears, and Mary Will had sailed for Shanghai and her wedding.

It has happened to other girls, no doubt. Young Paige met her boat. He was very drunk, and there was in his face evidence of a fall to depths unspeakable. Poor Mary Will saw at the first frightened look that the boy she had known and loved was gone forever. Many of the other girls—helpless, without money, alone—marry the men and make the best of it. Not Mary Will. Helpless, without money, alone, she was still brave enough to hold her head high and refuse.

Henry Drew had heard of her plight and, whatever his motive, had done a kind act for once. He engaged Mary, Will as companion for his wife, and on the boat coming over the girl and Mrs. Drew had occupied a cabin with a frail little missionary woman. For husbands and wives were ruthlessly torn apart, that each stateroom might have its full quota of three. As I sat there with the fog dripping down upon me I pictured again our good-bye on the deck, where we had been lined up to await the port doctor and be frisked, as a frivolous ship's officer put it, for symptoms of yellow fever. By chance—more or less—I was waiting beside Mary Will.

"Too bad you can't see the harbor," said Mary Will. "Only six weeks ago I sailed away, and the sun was on it. It's beautiful. But this silly old fog—"

"Never mind the fog," I told her. "Please listen to me. What are you going to do? Where are you going? Home?"

"Home!" A bitter look came into her clear blue eyes. "I can't go home."

"Why not?"

"Don't you understand? There were showers—showers for the bride-to-be. And I kissed everybody good-bye and hurried away to be married. Can I go back husbandless?"

"You don't have to. I told you last night—"

"I know. In the moonlight, with the band on the boat deck playing a waltz. You said you loved me—"

"And I do."

She shook her head.

"You pity me. And it seems like love to you. But pity—pity isn't love."

Confound the girl! This was her story, and she seemed determined to stick to it.

"Ah, yes," said I scornfully. "What pearls of wisdom fall from youthful lips."

"You'll discover how very wise I was in time."

"Perhaps. But you haven't answered my question. What are you going to do? You can't stay on with the Drews—that little rotter—"

"I know. He hasn't been nice to you. But he has been nice to me—very."

"No man could help but be. And it hasn't done that young wife of his any harm to have a companion like you for a change. But it's not a job I care to see held by the girl I mean to marry."

"If you mean me—I shan't go on being a companion. Mr. Drew has promised to find me a position in San Francisco. They say it's a charming city."

"I don't like to see you mixed up with Drew and his kind," I protested. "I'll not leave San Francisco until you do."

"Then you're going to settle down here. How nice!"

I could have slapped her. She was that sort of stubborn delightful child, and loving her was often that sort of emotion. The port doctor had reached her now in his passage down the line, and he stared firmly into her eyes, hunting symptoms. As he stared his hard face softened into a rather happy smile. I could have told him that looking into Mary Will's eyes had always that effect.

"You're all right," he laughed, then turned and glared at me as though he dared me to make public his lapse into a human being. He went on down the line. After him came Parker, the ship's doctor, with a wink at me, as much as to say: "Red tape. What a bore!"

The foghorn was making a frightful din, and the scene was all confusion, impatience. It was no moment for what I was about to say. But I was desperate; this was my last chance.

"Turn round, Mary Will." I swung her about and pointed off into the fog. "Over there—don't you see?"

"See what?" she gasped.

"How I love you," I said in her ear, triumphing over the foghorn and the curiosity of the woman just beyond her: "With all my heart and soul, my dear. I'm an engineer—not up on sentimental stuff—can't talk it—just feel it. Give me a chance to prove how much I care. Don't you think that in time—"

She shook her head.

"What is it? Are you still fond of that other boy—the poor fellow in Shanghai?"

"No," she answered seriously. "It isn't that. I've just sort of buried him away off in a corner of my heart. And I'm not sure that I ever did care as much as I should. On the boat coming out—I had doubts of myself—but—"

"But what?"

"Oh—can't you see? It's just as that old dowager said it would be."

"What old dowager?"

"That sharp-tongued Englishwoman who gave the dinner in Shanghai. She saw you talking and laughing with me, and she said: 'I fancy he'll be just like all the other boys who are shut up in China for a few years. They think themselves madly in love with the first white girl they meet who isn't positively deformed.'"

"The old cat!"

"It was catty—but it was true. It's exactly what has happened. That's why I couldn't be so frightfully unfair to you as to seize you when this madness is on you and bind you to me for life—before you have seen your own country again, where there are millions of girls nicer than I am."

"Rot."

"No, it isn't. Go ashore and look them over. The streets of San Francisco are filled with them. Look them over from the Golden Gate to Fifth Avenue."

"And if, after I've looked them all over, I still come back to you? Then what?"

"Then you will be a fool," laughed Mary Will.

The voice of the ship's doctor announced the end of inspection, and at once the deck was alive with an excited throng, all seeking to get somewhere else immediately. Carlotta Drew passed and called to Mary Will.

The girl held out her hand. "Good-bye," she said.

"Good-bye?" I took her hand perplexed. "Why do you say that? Surely we're to meet again soon."

"Why should we?" she asked.

That hurt me. I dropped her hand. "Ah, yes, why should we?" I repeated coldly.

"No reason at all. Good-bye and good luck!" And Mary Will was gone.

As I sat now on my battered bags, leaning against a very damp pole in the middle of a very damp fog, it occurred to me that I had been wrong in permitting myself that moment of annoyance. I should have taken, instead, a firm uncompromising attitude. Too late now, however. She had gone from me, into the mystery of the fog. I would never see her again.

A tall slender figure loaded with baggage came and stood on the curb not two feet from where I waited. The light that struggled down from a lamp overhead revealed in blurred but unmistakable outline the flat expressionless face of Hung Chin-chung, old Henry Drew's faithful body servant. I turned, for the master could not be far behind, and sure enough the fog disgorged the dapper figure of the little millionaire. He ran smack into me.

"Why, it's young Winthrop," he cried, peering into my face. "Hello, son—I was looking for you. We've had some pretty harsh words—but there's no real reason why we shouldn't part as friends. Now, is there?"

His tone was wistful, but it made no appeal to me. No real reason? The presumptuous rascal! However, I was in no mood to quarrel.

"I'm waiting for a taxi," I said inanely,

"A taxi? You'll never get one in this fog." I suppose it was the truth. "Let us give you a lift to your hotel, my boy. We'll be delighted."

I was naturally averse to accepting favors of this man, but at that instant his wife and Mary Will emerged into our little circle of light, and I smiled at the idea of riding uptown with Mary Will, who had just dismissed me for all time. A big limousine with a light burning faintly inside slipped up to the curb, and Hung was helping the women to enter.

"Come on, my boy," pleaded old Drew.

"All right," I answered rather ungraciously, and jumped in.

Drew followed, Hung piled my bags somewhere in back, and we crept off into the fog.

"Taking Mr. Winthrop to his hotel," explained Drew.

"How nice," his wife said in her cold hard voice. I looked toward Mary Will. She seemed unaware of my presence.

Like a living thing, the car felt its way cautiously through the mist. About us sounded a constant symphony of automobile horns, truckmen's repartee, the clank of hoofs, the rattle of wheels. From where I sat I could see the clear-cut beautiful silhouette of Carlotta Drew's face, shrouded in fog, against the window. I wondered what she was thinking—this woman whose exploits had furnished the gossips of the China coast with a serial story running through many mad years. Of her first husband, perhaps; that gallant army man whose heart she had soon broken as she leapt to the arms of another. They had come and gone, the men, until, her beauty fading, she had accepted the offer of old Drew's millions, though she hated him in her heart. What a fool the old man had been! On our trip across the gossips had played once more with her rather frail reputation, linking her name with that of the ship's doctor, handsome hero of many a fleeting romance.

"Home again," chuckled old Drew. An unaccustomed gaiety seemed to have taken hold of him. "I tell you, it's good. This is my town. This is where I belong. The history of our family, my boy, is woven into the story of San Francisco. By the way— what I wanted to see you about. Er—I want to ask a favor."

He stopped. I said nothing. A favor of me! One had to admire his nerve.

"It is nothing much," he went on. "Only—I'm giving a little dinner party tonight. A birthday party, as a matter of fact. I'd like to have you come. One of my guests will be my partner in the mine. We can talk over that little matter of business."

"Hardly the time or the place," I suggested.

This was like him. A gay party—plenty to eat and drink— and my affair hastily disposed of amid the general conviviality. I was not to be trapped like that.

"Well, perhaps not," he admitted. "We won't talk business, then. Just a gay little party—to brighten up the old house—to get things going in a friendly way again. Eh, Carlotta?"

"Oh, of course," said Carlotta Drew wearily.

"You'll come?" the old man insisted. I have often wondered since why he was so eager. He had wronged me, he knew, but he was that type of man who wishes to be on friendly terms with his victim. A plentiful type.

"I'm sure Miss Mary Will wishes you to accept," he added.

"She hasn't said so," I said.

"It's not my birthday," said Mary Will, "nor my party."

"Not your birthday," cackled old Drew. "I should say not. But your party, I hope. Everybody's party. What do you say, my boy?"

Mary Will's indifference had maddened me, and nothing could keep me from that party now.

"I'll be delighted to come," I said firmly. It was to Drew I spoke, but my gaze was on Mary Will's scornful profile.

"That's fine!" cried the old man. He peered out the window. "Where are we? Ah, yes—Post and Grant—there's a shop near here." He ordered his chauffeur to stop. "I'll be only a minute," he said as the car drew up to the curb. "Must have candles—candles for my party." And he hopped out. We stood there in the fog with the Wagnerian symphony fierce about us. It was after five now, and all San Francisco, to say nothing of Oakland and Berkeley, was stumbling home through the murk.

"Your husband seems in a gay humor tonight," I remarked to Carlotta Drew. She nodded, but said nothing. "Probably the effect of San Francisco," I went on. "I've always heard of it as a merry town. Life and color and romance—"

"And dozens of beautiful girls," put in Mary Will.

"I don't see them."

"Wait till the fog lifts," she answered.

Henry Drew was again at the door. He ordered the driver to stop at my hotel, then popped back into his seat. In his hand he carried a small package.

"Candles for the party," he laughed. "Fifty little pink candles."

Fifty! I stared at him there in that dim-lit car. Fifty—why, the old boy must be seventy if he was a day. Did he hope by this silly ruse to win back his middle age, in our eyes at least? Or wait a minute! Was he only fifty, after all? If rumor were true, he had lived a wild, reckless life. Perhaps that life had played a trick upon him—had made his fifty look like seventy.

We drew up before my hotel, and Hung Chin-chung was instantly on the sidewalk with my bags.

"I'll send the car for you at seven," Drew said. "We'll have a merry party. Don't fail me."

I thanked him, and amid muttered *au revoirs* the car went on its way. Standing on the curb, I stared after it. This was incredible! My first night back on American soil, the night I had been dreaming of for four years—and I was to spend it celebrating the birthday of my bitterest enemy! But there was Mary Will. She had dismissed me forever, and I was bound to show her she could not do that.

CHAPTER III

A few minutes before seven I came downstairs into the bright lobby of my hotel. Parker, the ship's doctor, whose cabin Drew and I had shared on the way across, was lolling in a chair. He rose and came toward me, a handsome devil in evening clothes—indubitably handsome, indubitably a devil.

"All dolled up," he said.

"Going to a birthday party," I answered.

"Great Scott! You don't mean you're invited to old Drew's shindig?"

"Why shouldn't I be invited?" I asked.

"But you and the old man—you're deadly enemies—"

"Not at all. He rather likes me. Found me so easy to flim-flam—my type appeals to him. He pleaded with me to come."

"But you? You don't like him? Yet you accept. Ah, yes—I was forgetting the little southern girl—"

"My reasons," I said hotly, "happen to be my own affair."

"Naturally." His tone was conciliatory. "Come and have a drink. No? I am going to the party myself."

I had been wondering—his fame as a philanderer was international. Was this affair with Carlotta Drew anything more than a passing flurry to relieve the tedium of another trip across? Here was the answer. Evidently it was.

"Fearful bore," he went on. "But Carlotta insisted. I'd do anything for Carlotta Drew. Wonderful woman!"

"Think so?" said I.

"Don't you?" he asked.

"In the presence of an expert," said I, "I would hesitate to express an opinion."

He laughed.

"Er—you know something of old Drew's affairs," he ventured. "Must be a very rich man?"

"Must be," said I.

"That mine you worked in? Big money maker?"

"Big money maker." I repeated his words intentionally. He was frank, at any rate. What cruel thoughts were stirring behind those green eyes? Henry Drew out of the way, Carlotta with the added charm of millions.

"But he's only fifty," I said as unkindly as I could.

"Only fifty?"

"Sure—the party," I explained.

Parker shook his head.

"Looks more than fifty to me," he said quite hopefully.

Hung Chin-chung, a strange figure in that Occidental lobby, stood suddenly before me, bowing low. Drew's car was waiting, he said.

"Want to ride up with me?" I inquired of Parker.

"Er—no, thanks. I'll drop in later. Have some matters to attend to. So long!"

He headed for the bar, where the matters no doubt awaited his attention. I accompanied the Chinaman out of the lobby and once more entered the Drew limousine. Following the faint whir of an expensive motor, again we were abroad in the fog-bound street.

The traffic so much in evidence at five o'clock was no more, the grumbling symphony was stilled, and only the doubtful honk-honk of an occasional automobile broke the silence. Inside the car the light was no longer on, and I sat in a most oppressive darkness. Almost immediately we began to ascend a very steep incline. Nob Hill, no doubt, famous in the history of this romantic, climbing town. Eagerly I pressed my face against the pane beside me, but the tule-fog still blotted out the city of my dreams.

At one corner we grazed the side of some passing vehicle, and loud curses filled the air. I found the switch and flooded the interior of the car with light. It fell on the gray upholstery, on the silver handles of the doors. I was reminded of something—something unpleasant. Ah, yes—a coffin. I switched off the light again.

After a ride of some twenty minutes we drew up beside the curb, and Hung stood waiting for me at the door. Back of him was vaguely outlined a monster of a house, with yellow lights fighting their way through the tule-fog from many windows.

"The end of our journey," said Hung. "If you will deign to come, please."

I followed him up many steps. Henry Drew must have heard us, for he was waiting in the doorway.

"Fine! Fine!" cried the old man.

"Delighted to see you. Come right in. The house is a bit musty—been closed for a long time."

It was musty. Though I came from the clammy gloom of a tule-fog, I was struck at once with a feeling of chill and staleness and age. Despite the many lights blazing inside, I thought this house would always be musty with the accumulation of many years. For it was very old, it had escaped the fire, and here it stood with its memories, waiting for the wrecker, Time, to write *Finis* to its history.

"Hung—take Mr. Winthrop's hat and coat." Old Drew seized me almost affectionately by the arm. "You come with me." He was like a small boy celebrating his first real birthday party. He led me into a library lined with dusty books. From the walls, San Francisco Drews, blond and brunette, lean and fat, old and young, looked down on us. "Take that chair by the fire, my boy."

I sat down. There was something depressing in the air, there was much that was pathetic about Henry Drew. His birthday! Who gave a hang? Certainly not his wife, who looked at him through eyes that seemed to be counting his years with ever-increasing hate; nor, probably, the son by his first marriage, whom I had never seen, but who, according to report, hated him too.

He went over and held those cold transparent hands of his up to the fire. I noticed that they trembled slightly.

"The girls will be down soon," he said. "Before they come I want to tell you that I've been thinking over our little matter—"

"Please," I interrupted. "I'm sure your party will go off much more pleasantly if there is no mention of that." I paused. "My lawyer will call on you tomorrow."

The shadow of a smile crossed his face. And well he might smile, for he knew that I was bluffing; I had no lawyer; I had, in fact, no case against him. "You're quite right, my boy," he said. "Tonight is no time for business. Let us eat, drink, and be merry, for tomorrow—tomorrow, I see your lawyer."

He laughed outright now, an unkind sneering laugh, and once more hatred of him blazed in my heart. Why had I been such a fool as to come?

The doorbell rang, a loud peal, and Drew ran to the hall, where Hung Chin-chung was already opening the outer door. Through the curtains I saw a huge rosy-cheeked policeman outlined against the fog.

"Hello, Mr. Drew," he said cheerily.

"Hello, Riley," cried the old man. Running forward he seized the policeman's hand. "I'm back again."

"And glad I am to see you," said Riley. "I knew the house was closed, and seein' all the lights, I thought I'd look in and make sure everything was okay."

"We landed late today," replied Drew. "Everything is certainly okay. You'll see plenty of lights here from now on."

He stood on the threshold, chatting gaily with the patrolman. Hung Chin-chung came into the library where I sat and, taking up a log, stooped to put it on the fire. The flicker of light played on his face, old, lined, yellow like a lemon left too long in the sun, and glinted in those dark inscrutable little eyes.

Drew sent Riley on his way with a genial word and returned to the library. Hung stood awaiting him, evidently about to speak.

"Yes, yes—what is it?" Drew asked.

"With your permission," said Hung, "I will go to my room."

"All right," Drew answered. "But be back here in half an hour. You're to serve dinner, you know."

"I will serve it," said Hung, and he went noiselessly out.

"What was I saying?" Drew turned to me. "Ah, yes—the girls—the girls will be down in a minute. Bless them! That Little Mary Will—like a breath of springtime from her own mountains. Ah, youth—youth! All I have gained, all that I have—I'd swap it tonight for youth. My boy, you don't know what you've got."

I stared at him. *He'll steal your shirt, and you'll beg him to take the pants too.* Thus inelegantly had old Drew been described to me in China, and there was some truth in it, surely. Where was my hatred of a moment ago? Confound it, there was something likable about him after all.

I stared at him no longer, for now outside the curtains I could see Mary Will coming down the stairs. Many beautiful women had come down those stairs in the days when social history was making in that old house on Nob Hill—women whose loveliness was now but a fast-fading memory on peeling canvas. But none, I felt quite certain, was fairer than Mary Will. The lights shone softly on her red-brown hair and on those white shoulders that were youth incarnate. She was wearing—well, I can't describe it, but it was unquestionably the very dress she should have worn. Thank God she had it and had put it on! She came into the library, and all the gloom and staleness fled.

"My dear—my dear!" Henry Drew met her, his eyes alight with admiration. "You are a picture, and no mistake. You carry me back—indeed you do—back to the time when these rooms were alive with youth and beauty." He waved a hand to the portrait of a woman in the post of honor above the fireplace. "You are very like her. My first wife, you know." He stood for a moment, pathetic, unhappy, weighed down by the years. more human than I had ever seen him before. "I don't imagine you two will object to being left alone," he said finally, attempting a smile. "I'm going to have a look at the table. Want everything just right." He crossed the hall and disappeared.

"Well, Mary Will—here I am," I announced.

"Sure enough," smiled Mary Will.

"This afternoon," said I, "at four o'clock, you put me out of your life forever. Twice since then I've popped back. And I'll go on popping, and popping, until you're a sweet gray-haired old lady, so you might as well take me and have done."

"Too bad," mused Mary Will, "about the fog. If you could have seen all those other girls—"

"Don't want to see them," I said firmly, "Tell me, how do you like it here in the family vault?"

She shuddered. "It's a bit oppressive. I'm going to strike out for myself tomorrow. Mr. Drew gave me a check tonight—I can live on that until I get a job."

"The cost of living is frightfully high."

"But worth it—don't you think?" she asked.

"With you—undoubtedly."

"You just keep going round in circles," she complained.

"You've got me going round in circles," I laughed. I came close to her before the fire. "Mary Will—I've never been in San Francisco before. And I've never been married. Two new experiences. I'd like to tackle them together. Tomorrow, after the fog lifts, and I've seen and rejected all the other girls, I'll meet you with a license in my pocket."

"Oh, dear—you are so sudden."

"It's girls like you that make men sudden."

"I never gave you any encouragement, I'm sure," she protested.

"You let me look at you. Encouragement enough."

"Look at me—and pity me."

"Now don't start that. It's love!"

"No—pity."

"Love, I fell you."

This might have gone on indefinitely, but suddenly Carlotta Drew's voice broke in, calling, and Mary Will fled, just as I had nearly got her hand. She fled, and that dim room was instantly old and stale again.

I stood alone with the past. My thoughts were most jumbled, chaotic. Drews—Drews innumerable—were looking down at me, wondering, perhaps, about this stranger who dared make love in the very room where they themselves had laughed and loved in the old far days. Wonderful days that glittered with the gold men were extracting from California's soil. Gone now, forever. And lovely ladies, turned to dust. Ugh—unpleasant thought! Look at the windows. Need washing, don't they? Or is it the heavy yellow fog from the tule-fields, pressing close against the paces, trying to get in? Quiet—oppressively quiet—what has become of everybody? No sound save the slow deliberate clicking of the big clock in the hallway. The voice of Time, who had conquered all these people on the wall. "I'll—get—you—too. "I'll—get—you—too." Was the clock really saying that? All right—some day, perhaps—but not yet. Now I had youth. "My boy, you don't know what you've got." Oh, yes, I do. Youth—and Mary Will. She, too, must be mine. She had looked wonderful. Where was she? Was I to be left alone forever with the confounded clock?

Suddenly from across the hall came a cry, sharp, uncanny, terrible. I ran out in the direction from which it had come and stood on the threshold of the Drew dining room. Another room of many memories, of stern faces on the wall. A table was set with gleaming silver and white linen, and in its center stood a cake, on which fifty absurd pink candles flickered bravely.

There appeared to be no one in the room. On the other side of the table a French window stood open to the fog, and I went around to investigate. I had taken perhaps a dozen steps when I stopped, appalled.

Old Drew was lying on the carpet, and one yellow lean hand, always so adept at reaching out and seizing, held a corner of the white tablecloth. There was a dark stain on the left side of his dress coat; and when I pulled the coat back, I saw on the otherwise spotless linen underneath a great red circle that grew and grew. He was quite dead.

I stood erect, and for a dazed uncertain moment I stared about the room. Beside me, on the table, fifty yellow points of flame trembled like human things terrified at what they had seen.

CHAPTER IV

As I stood there with Henry Drew's dead body at my feet and those silly candles flaring wanly at my side, I heard the big clock in the hallway strike the half hour, and then the scurry of feet on the stairs. Cleared now of its first amazement, my mind was unusually keen. Henry Drew done for at last! By whom? Again my eye fell upon the open French window and, stepping to it, I looked out. My heart stopped beating—for amid the shadows and the fog I thought I saw a blacker shadow, which passed in the twinkling of an eye.

I stepped quickly from the room. The light from the window at my back penetrated a few feet only on a narrow veranda, from which steps led down into a garden, I judged. It was unexplored country to me, the dark was impenetrable, but I stepped off into tall damp grass almost to my knees.

The tule-fog seemed glad to have me back. Its clammy embrace was about my ankles; from the bare branches of the trees above, it dripped down on my defenseless head. I took several steps to the right, and ran into an unexpected ell of the house. As I stood there, uncertain which way to go, something brushed against my face, something rough, uncanny, that sent a shiver down my spine. Wildly I swung my arms in all directions, but they touched only empty air and fog.

Still swinging my arms, stumbling amid flower beds, hunting in vain for a path, I continued to explore. My feet caught in a tangle of vines, and I came near sprawling on the wet grass. Righting myself with difficulty, I stopped and looked about me. The light from the room I had left was no longer visible. I was lost in a jungle that was only the Drew back yard. For a moment, I stood tense and silent. How I knew it I can not say, but I was conscious that I was not alone. Close at hand some human creature waited, holding its breath, alert, prepared. I did not see, I did not hear—I felt. Suddenly I lunged in the direction where I imagined it to be—and instantly my intuition was proved correct. I heard someone back away, and then quick heavy footsteps crunched on a gravel walk.

He had shown me the path, and for that I thanked him. Following as speedily as I could in his wake, I came to a gate in the high wall at the rear. It was swinging open. Through this, no doubt, the murderer had gone, and I stepped out into the alley. I could see no one; there was no sound whatever. Then I started and almost cried aloud—but it was only an alley cat brushing against my legs.

My quarry had vanished into the fog, and to look for him would be to hunt the proverbial needle in the good old haystack. It came to me then that I had been all kinds of a fool, rushing out of the Drew house like that at the moment of my gruesome discovery. I had not meant to come so far, of course—but here I was, and there was nothing to do but hurry back. How about Mary Will? Had she, perhaps, been the second person to enter the dining room and been frightened half to death by what she found there?

I swung back to reenter the garden—and at that instant the gate banged shut in my face. The wind? Nonsense, there was no wind. With a sickening sense of being tricked, I put my hand on the knob. I turned and pushed. As I expected, the gate was securely locked on the inside.

What should I do now? Wait here at the gate, holding my friend of the fog a prisoner inside? Useless, I reflected; there must be many ways of escape—a neighbor's yard on either side. Before I had waited five minutes, he would be well on his way to safety. No—I must get back to the house as quickly as I could. Since I could not return by way of the garden, only one course remained—I must follow the alley until I came to a cross-street, then travel that until I came to the street where

Henry Drew's house stood. But what was the name of the street where it stood?

All at once I realized that I hadn't the faintest idea. No matter, I must get back to that front door somehow. A short distance down, an alley lamp made an odd shape in the fog. I hurried toward it. Just beyond I stepped out into the cross-street and paused. Left or right? Left, of course.

The clammy yellow fog stuck closer than a brother. On my feet I wore patent leather shoes, recently purchased on my return to human society in Shanghai. Their soles were almost as they had been when I left the shop, and I slipped and skidded unmercifully on the damp sidewalk. A small matter—but one that somehow filled me with a feeling of helplessness and rage. What a spectacle I must present! Served me right, though. I had no business at Henry Drew's confounded party.

As best I could, I hurried on, staring at the house- fronts. But their owners couldn't have told them apart in the mist. My search was hopeless. I had given up and was standing beneath a street lamp when I heard footsteps.

Debonairly out of the fog walked Parker, the ship's doctor, humming a tune as he walked. He stopped and stared at me. A fine sight I must have been, too—wild-eyed, with evening clothes, no overcoat, no hat.

"Good lord, Winthrop!" he said. "What's happened to you?"

There was no friendliness in his tone, and it came to me suddenly—a sickening premonition—that this was the last man it was good for me to meet just now. I resolved to make the best of my plight.

"Parker, a terrible thing has happened. Old man Drew has been murdered."

"You don't say? Who killed him?"

"I don't know. How the devil should I?" His cool unconcerned tones maddened me. "I had reached the house, and was waiting for him in the library. Hearing a cry, I ran into the diningroom. He was there—dead—on the floor."

"Really? And now you are wildly, running the streets. Hunting for a policeman, perhaps?"

I was not unaware of the sneering implication in his words, but I strove to keep my temper.

"I'm trying to get back to the house," I said calmly. "As I was standing beside the old man's body I saw someone moving outside an open window."

I outlined briefly the series of small adventures that had followed. He heard me out, then tossed away his cigarette, and I saw a faint smile on his cruel face. It occurred to me that I would have to repeat my story—repeat it again and again—and that I was destined to see that smile of unbelief on other faces.

"Very interesting," said Parker, still smiling. "I wish I could be of some help, old man. But as a matter of fact I'm in the same fix as you. I started to walk to the house, and lost my way."

"At any rate," I answered, "you must know the address."

"Don't you?" He laughed loudly. "I say, that's funny."

"To you, perhaps," I said.

"Pardon me. My sense of humor breaks out at most unseemly times. I do know the address, of course. The house is on California Street." He mentioned a number.

"There are no street signs on the lamps," I said.

"No. But at each corner the name of the street is carved in the sidewalk. Let's try that."

We walked along to the nearest crossing. Neither of us had a match; but by stooping and running his fingers along the damp walk Parker came upon the name carved in the stone. I leaned over beside him, and we began to spell it out. It was in such a silly posture that Riley the policeman found us as his big bulk emerged from the fog.

"What the hell?" said Riley, not without reason.

"It's Riley!" I cried. "Good enough!"

"Who are you?" he wanted to know.

"A friend of Mr. Drew," I told him. "I was there a while ago when you called to see if everything was okay."

"Sure," he said "You was sitting in the library."

"Of course. Riley—Mr. Drew has bees murdered."

"Murdered! He can't be. I was just talkin' to him."

I told him of the events since his call at the Drew house, and repeated the lame story of my actions following my discovery of the crime. He made no comment.

"How about you?" he said, turning to Parker.

"I met this young man by chance,' Parker told him. "I was on my way to Mr. Drew's house, where I had been invited for dinner, and I became confused in the fog."

Riley shook his head.

"I don't mind sayin' you both sound fishy to me," he remarked. "We'll go back to the house. You lads follow me—wait a bit. Second thoughts is best. You lead the way."

He pointed with his night stick, and meekly we set out. Riley pounded along at our heels. We must have been far afield, for we walked some distance, passing several corners where motorcars honked dubiously. At last Riley halted us before the Drew house, and we climbed the steps. Finding the door unlocked, we entered with Riley close behind.

CHAPTER V

The life of the Drew household appeared to be at the moment centered in the great hall into which we came. Carlotta Drew was lying back on a big sofa at the left, indulging in the luxury of mild hysterics, and Mary Will bent over her, a bottle of smelling salts in her hand. A little old woman with a kindly face, evidently a servant, was weeping silently near the stairs, and at the moment of our entrance, Hung Chin-chung emerged from the dining room with no sign of emotion on his inscrutable face.

"Mary Will," I said gently.

She lifted her head and looked at me. There was terror in her eyes, but at sight of me it appeared to give way to an intense relief.

"You've come back," she said, as though in surprise. "Oh— I'm so glad you've come back."

At the moment I did not understand the full meaning of her words. Carlotta Drew sat up at sight of Doctor Parker and abandoned her mechanical exhibition of grief. Perhaps she remembered the effect of tears on even the most careful makeup.

"Now, what's it all about?" boomed Riley. "Mrs. Mac-Shane—" He turned to the old servant.

"The poor man!" wept Mrs. MacShane. "In there—in the dining room—"

"Has anyone called the station?"

"Sure, I called 'em," said the old woman, evidently efficient even under stress.

"They'll be sendin' a detective over," said Riley. "No one leaves—that's understood."

He passed on into the tragic room where the candles were burning. Hurrying to Mary Will's side, I began once more the tale of my adventures since finding the millionaire's body. As I spoke in a low voice I thought she looked at me in an odd way. My heart sank. Was even Mary Will going to doubt my story?

Riley returned.

"It's hard to realize, Mrs. MacShane," he said. "He was a kind man—you know that. Many's the time, on cold nights, he had me in from the misty streets for a drop—but no matter."

There was a brisk knock at the front door, and a figure muffled in a huge coat stepped into the hall. Close behind came two policemen in uniform. At sight of the figure leading the way, Riley was all respect.

"Sergeant Barnes—you are needed here," he said.

"Yes!"

The voice of Detective Sergeant Barnes rang out sharp and alive and vital in that house of dim shadows and far memories. He slipped off coat and hat and tossed them down on a chair. I saw that he was a cool, quick little man, bald of head, unsympathetic of eye, business from the word go.

"Henry Drew?" he snapped.

Riley nodded. "In the dining room—about forty minutes ago," he said.

"Myers!" Detective Barnes turned to one of the uniformed men. "You take the front. Murphy—the back door for you." The two men left for their posts. Barnes stood, staring about the room. "Drew had a son. Mark Drew—lawyer—Athletic Club. I don't see him here."

"He's on his way, sir," said Mrs. MacShane. "I called him. Sure, I thought of him right away, though why I did I don't know, for not in five years has he set foot in this house—"

"All right," the detective cut her short. He was still studying that odd little group: Parker, sneering, unmoved; Carlotta Drew, shaken a bit in the face of a consummation she had no doubt long desired; Mary Will, young and innocent and lovely; the old Irish woman with the tears still wet on her cheeks; and the yellow Chinaman standing patient as a beast of burden by the stairs. And finally he looked at me, whose enemy lay low at last beside the fifty candles.

"No one leaves this house until I have completed my investigation," he announced. "You stay here, Riley, and see to that."

"Yes, sir," said Riley, with a determined look about our circle. Sergeant Barnes strode into the dining room.

"A merry party—to brighten up the old house—to get things going in a friendly way again." The words of the old millionaire spoken in his car as we rode uptown came back to me. How different, this, from the party Henry Drew had planned! No one spoke. Each sat wrapped in gloomy thought under the glare of Riley. Only one sound broke the stillness—the voice of Time in the person of the clock, still ticking its eternal threat.

Mary Will sat not three feet from me, but I had the feeling that she was miles away. Some sudden barrier seemed to have arisen between us. She glanced toward me but seldom, and when she did it was with a look in her eyes I did not like to see. I was glad when the loud peal of the doorbell broke the stillness of the room.

Mrs. MacShane opened the door, and a brisk good-looking man of about thirty-five came in. The old woman's first words identified him.

"Oh, Mr. Mark," she cried. "Your poor father!"

So this was Mark Drew. There was none of his father's shrewd, wicked cunning in his eyes as he gazed frankly about the room. His face was a pleasant one, wrinkled with the evidence of much smiling. No wonder this man and his cruel old father had come in time to the parting of the ways.

Carlotta Drew stepped forward and held out her hand. "I am Carlotta. Your father's wife. We have never met."

He made no move to take her hand.

"I have heard about you," he said gravely and moved on, leaving her standing foolishly with her hand outstretched.

The wave of hatred that passed over her face was not pretty to see, but she tossed her head and with a hard little laugh resumed her seat. Mark Drew went on instinctively to the dining room, and we heard his voice and that of the detective as they conversed together. Then the voices grew fainter, a window slammed; they had moved on into the garden.

After an interval Drew and the detective came back into the hall. The former sat down, his face in his hands, and Barnes stood in the center of our group playing with a little pack of white cards in his hand.

"Well—let's get acquainted," he began. "How many of you were in the house when this thing happened?"

All save Parker admitted their presence.

"Was there any noise—any sound—from that room?"

"Yes," I told him. "There was a cry—a sharp, rather terrible scream. I was in the library, waiting for—er—him. I ran into the dining room. The table was set—the cake with fifty candles on it."

Mark Drew raised his head. "Sergeant, in regard to those fifty candles—" he began.

"Yes," said Barnes. "Let that pass for now. You—go on. You went into the room. You were the first to enter."

"Undoubtedly. Mr. Drew was lying on the floor on the other side of the table, not far from the open window. He was dead— stabbed just below the heart."

"Did you notice a knife or any other weapon?"

"I didn't look for one. The open window caught my eye, and when I stepped to it I thought I saw someone in the garden."

The moment I had been dreading had come, and I pulled myself together. Once more I must relate my story, and this time the manner of its acceptance was vital to me. I told of the figure in the garden, the footsteps on the gravel, the gate that had been slammed and locked behind me. I pictured myself lost in the fog, trying to return to the house. Though I put forth every effort to make it sound reasonable, it didn't; it sounded silly, preposterous. I felt Mary Will's eyes upon me. The detective gave no sign.

"Before I ask you how you got back here," he said, "I want to say—I don't get you. Who are you? What's your position here? A friend of Henry Drew?"

"Decidedly not. I was an employee."

"Decidedly not? What do you mean by that?"

"If I may speak," drawled Carlotta Drew. She stared at me between narrowed lids, cold, calculating, hostile. "If I may speak, I think I can throw some light on that. This young man was employed by my husband in the Yunnan mines, and he claimed he bad been unfairly treated. There was some cock-and-bull story about a promise—"

"There was a promise," I said, "and it was no cock-and-bull story."

"He had quarreled violently with my husband, who dismissed him."

"That's not true," I said. "I resigned."

"By chance they occupied the same cabin on the boat coming from China, along with Doctor Parker here," the woman went on. "I believe the quarreling continued." She looked questioningly at Parker.

"It did," the doctor said. "For several days after they came aboard. I'll swear to that. Then they stopped speaking to each other."

"And yet—" Barnes turned to me. "You were a guest at dinner?"

"Yes," I said. "I believe that for some reason Drew wanted to smooth the matter out. He suggested I come here to meet his partner in the mines, Doctor Su Yen Hun, a Chinese merchant in this town. I agreed to come, but I told him I'd rather not discuss business."

"If you didn't want to talk business, why did you come?"

"I came because—" I stopped. But I was resolved to tell the truth from start to finish. "I came because I wished to see again Mrs. Drew's companion, Miss Tellfair."

The detective's eyes followed mine and rested on Mary Will. "Huh! You're interested in the young lady?"

"I've asked her to marry me," I told him.

"Yeah. You admit, then, that there had been bad blood between you and Henry Drew over business matters? You claim he cheated you?"

"I do."

"We left you wandering in the fog, trying to get back to this house, you say. You got back. How?"

"I met this gentleman—Doctor Parker. He had been invited here to dinner and was walking up from his hotel. He claimed that he, too, was lost."

"Doctor Parker?" Barnes turned and surveyed him.

"Yes," said the doctor, smiling his devilishly mean smile. "I met this young man wandering in the fog. I must say he had a wild look about him, but that, of course, is unimportant. Truth compels me to add that he was going at a rather rapid gait away from the house."

"How did you know, if you were lost yourself?" Barnes asked.

"It was later proved when we met Officer Riley and he showed us the way." I saw the eyes of Parker and Carlotta Drew meet then, and I knew without further proof that a partnership had been formed to fasten this crime on me, if possible. But why? There could be but one reason, and I was startled as it flashed into my mind. Where was Doctor Parker at a little before seven-thirty? Lost in the fog—alone.

Detective Barnes turned again to Carlotta Drew.

"Now, Mrs. Drew," he began, "please tell me what you were doing at half past seven o'clock?"

"I was in my room, dressing for dinner," she said. "Miss Tellfair, my companion, was with me. I have no maid at present, and I had called her up to assist me with some troublesome hooks in the back. We were together there when we heard the cry."

"You heard a cry. What then?"

"My heart stood still. I tried to speak, but I couldn't."

Mary Will turned suddenly and faced her.

"I beg your pardon," she said. "Your memory is slightly at fault. You had no difficulty in speaking. In fact, you spoke distinctly."

"Nonsense! I don't remember."

"I do," replied Mary Will firmly. "You said quite clearly, 'He's done it! He's done it!' You said it twice."

"He's done it?" repeated Barnes. "Just what, Mrs. Drew, did you mean by that?"

"If I said it at all," answered Carlotta Drew icily, "which I doubt, I do not know what I meant. I was beside myself with terror."

"But why should you be beside yourself with terror, as you say? You had no means of knowing what that cry meant."

"I knew only too well. My dear husband's life had been threatened—only recently, as a matter of fact—by Mr. Winthrop here."

"I deny that," said I.

"Did you hear Mr. Winthrop threaten your husband—my father?" asked Mark Drew sharply.

"No-o," said the woman. "Not precisely. But Henry—Mr. Drew—had told me he was afraid of Mr. Winthrop. He was very much upset when he found himself in the same stateroom with him. He tried to be moved."

"Then when you cried out 'He's done. it,'" suggested Doctor Parker, "you were—almost unconsciously—thinking of Winthrop?"

"That must have been it."

"Doctor—you're invaluable," said Mark Drew with a strange smile.

"Come, come!" broke in Barnes. "Let's get on. You heard the cry?"

"Miss Tellfair ran out of the room," went on Carlotta Drew.

"I started to," corrected Mary Will, the color rising in her white cheeks. "But you held me back. You clung to me."

"I tell you I was beside myself. I didn't know what I was doing."

"You take it up," suggested Barnes to Mary Will.

"I managed to get away," Mary Will said, "and ran downstairs. I looked in the library; it was empty. The dining room door was open. I went in—"

"You were, then, the second person to enter the room?"

"Very likely." Mary Will's voice was low now—little more than a whisper. "I thought the room empty at first. The window stood open. I went round the table, and there—on the floor—I saw him—Mr. Drew."

"Yes—go on."

"I—I screamed and ran from the room."

"Ah, yes!" said Barnes. "Did you by any chance see a weapon of any sort—a knife, perhaps—near Mr. Drew's body?"

"I scarcely looked," answered Mary Will, her lovely eyes full on the detective's face. "I was so frightened, you understand—"

"Of course, of course. No matter,

Barnes said. "You screamed and ran from the room."

"Yes. In the doorway I met Mrs. MacShane. Mrs. Drew was coming down the stairs. She followed Mrs. MacShane into the dining room. In a moment she, too, screamed—and I believe she fainted in Mrs. MacShane's arms."

"It was almost a faint," said the old woman.

"Miss Tellfair, please," Barnes insisted.

"I knew where Mrs. Drew kept a bottle of smelling salts," Mary Will continued. "She had used them on the boat, and I'd packed them for her. I ran up and got them and brought them down. That's—that's all, I think." I fancied that Mary Will was near a faint herself.

"And now, Mrs. MacShane," said the detective, "we'll listen to you."

"Officer—my story's soon told," said the old woman. "I hears the cry, and bein' busy with dinner, ordered at the last minute, as ye might say, I didn't pay no attention. I'm no cook, I'm a caretaker, an' I was doin' the cookin' as a favor to poor Mr. Drew, who sint me the word by wireless today, I havin' looked after the house while he was away. 'Sure,' says I, 'that's a keen cry, an' a bitter one, but my business is here.' Thin I got to thinkin', so I took a minute to come trottin' in; after that it was as the young lady says. I found what I found…poor Mr. Drew—God rest his soul!"

The quick eye of Barnes once more traveled around that little group.

"Doctor Parker, I believe, was lost in the fog at half past seven on his way to the house," he said. "That leaves nobody but this stony-faced Chinaman. I'd as soon go out in the Sahara Desert and have a chat with the Sphinx as question one of 'em. Come here, you!"

Hung Chin-chung stiffened, and a dignity that was ever part of him shone from his strange eyes as he crossed the room and stood before the detective.

"What's your name?" roared Barnes. He was one of those Americans who believe all foreigners are deaf.

Hung stared at him in amiable contempt.

Mark Drew spoke up. "If I may make a suggestion," he said, "Hung was almost one of the family. He was my father's body-servant, for twenty years his best friend, and in these later years, I am afraid, his only friend. Hung's name, Chin-chung, means completely loyal, and he was all of that. He has never been known to refuse any request my father made of him, and I am sure my father was extremely fond of him. So was Hung fond of my father, and I am very much mistaken if, despite the lack of evidence in his face, Hung is not the sincerest mourner among us here tonight."

The Chinaman bowed.

"It is sweet indeed," he said in precise, perfect English, "if I have found such honor in the eyes of my employer's son. You are a policeman," he added, turning gravely on Barnes, "and you wish to know of my movements in this house tonight. When the matter under discussion was in progress, I was in my room, whither I had gone with my master's permission. This young man—" He nodded toward me. "—was in the room when that permission was granted."

"That's right," I said.

"I am no butler," Hung went on. "But we had only today arrived from China, and there was not yet time to engage a servant of that class. Mr. Drew had asked me to serve the dinner tonight, and I had agreed to do so, as I agreed to all his wishes, always. I was in my room making certain changes in my attire, that I might bring honor to my master and my master's house in the eyes of his friends."

"Did you hear anything?"

"My room," said Hung, "is on the fourth floor, at the rear. No sound of any disturbance reached my ears. I came down, prepared to serve dinner, and found the house in an uproar. My master, who was as dear to me as the bones of my honorable ancestors, was dead beside the table where dinner was prepared."

"There's a back stairs?" suggested Barnes.

"Ah, yes," replied Hung, "a back stairs, leading through the kitchen of Mrs. MacShane. If I had passed that way—"

"He didn't," said the old woman. "I never left the kitchen from five this afternoon till I come in here. I saw nothing of Hung. He speaks the truth."

Barnes stood staring at Hung through his vivid little eyes, but the eyes of the Chinaman gave back no answering gleam. Still the detective played with the pack of white cards in his hand.

"We're getting nowhere," pouted Carlotta Drew. "I must say I feel faint and weak. Surely we may be excused now."

"Not yet!" snapped Barnes. "I'm sorry. I believe you've had no dinner. If Mrs. MacShane here could make us all a cup of coffee—?"

"I can that," said Mrs. MacShane.

"Go and help," said Barnes to Hung, and the latter, after a moment of open defiance, turned slowly on his velvet- shod feet and followed the old woman to the kitchen.

Barnes stood in deep thought, looking from one to another of the group that remained. His eye as it met mine was cold and calculating, and I knew that if he could fix a semblance of guilt on my head, he would do it.

A man prominent in San Francisco life was murdered. There would be an outcry in the newspapers, and an arrest must be made to save the face of the police—the guilty man if possible; if not, someone who seemed guilty.

"Let's go back," he said with sudden decision. "Henry Drew was giving a birthday party tonight. I noticed, Mr. Drew, that when you saw the cake with the fifty candles you appeared surprised. I take it this was not your father's birthday."

"It most certainly was not," Mark Drew replied. "If you will consult the family Bible in the library, you will find that my father was born not in December, but in March. He was sixty-nine years old last March."

"Sixty-nine," mused Barnes. "Yet this was somebody's fiftieth birthday—somebody Henry Drew thought highly enough of to honor with a party. Whose birthday was it? Mrs. Drew—do you know?"

"I do not," said Carlotta Drew. "My husband confided few of his affairs to me."

"Yes? Well, I guess we can take it for granted that the person in whose honor the party was given was to be among the guests." Barnes held up the little pack of white cards. "I've got here the place cards for the party, which I gathered up from the table." Ile began to read. "Mr. Winthrop—you're not fifty. Miss

Tellfair—I don't need to ask. Doctor Parker—er—how about you?"

"Not guilty," Parker said. "It's not my birthday, and Mr. Drew wouldn't have given me a party if it were."

Barnes held up another card, and for a long moment gazed at the face of Carlotta Drew. He must have seen the lines and wrinkles that even the best of makeups could not completely hide.

"If you will pardon me, Mrs. Drew—"

"I have already told you," answered Carlotta Drew angrily, "I do not know whose birthday it is."

"Well, no offense," smiled Barnes. "That leaves me just one card—the card of the guest who for some reason or other has not come to the party, Doctor Su Yen Hun. The other partner in the Yunnan mine, I believe."

"So I understand," said I.

"Do you know him?"

"I met him four years ago in Shanghai."

"He was a partner in the fraud you claim was practiced on you?"

"I understand he was a partner in all of Drew's shady deals."

"An interesting guest. I'd like to see him." Barnes turned to the patrolman, who was still waiting. "Riley, before I let you go back to your beat, do this for me. Go to Su Yen Hun's house— you know, the big Chinese millionaire—it's just round the corner on Post Street. Give Su my compliments and ask him to step over here a minute."

"Yes, sir," said Riley and promptly disappeared.

"I can tell you in advance—this is not Su's fiftieth birthday," Mark Drew said. "He's a very old man—eighty or more."

"I know he is," Barnes answered, "but he's worth a question or two anyhow. Now while you people are waiting for your coffee, I'll have a look about the upstairs." He paused at the foot of the stairway. "Myers is in front, and Murphy's in the garden," he smiled. "Good men, both of them. So keep your seats."

As the detective walked briskly up the stairs, I was startled to see Mary Will's eyes following him, wide and frightened. I went quickly to her side, but before I could speak, Doctor Parker cut in.

"That is an outrage!" he cried. He rose and walked angrily up and down. "Why should I be held here? I came to this house for a party, not an inquest. When that fool detective comes back, I'm going to demand that he let me go."

Mark Drew answered in a low, surprisingly hostile tone. "I would not call that fool detective's attention to myself if I were you."

"What do you mean by that?" snarled Parker, turning on him.

"Lost in the fog," smiled Drew. "Not much of an alibi, Doctor, if you ask me."

"Do you dare to insinuate—"

"That you would injure my father? When have you ever done anything else?"

"I don't know what you're talking about."

"Oh, don't you? I mean you are too eager, my dear Doctor—you and this woman here—to fasten the crime on the head of a young man who may or may not be guilty. Don't think you can fool me. Don't think I can't read you—the pair of you. You have made the last years of my father's life a hell. And what does his death mean to you? This woman with a big share of my father's money—and no more need of secrecy. Take care, Doctor Parker. I'm telling you, the fog is a rotten alibi."

"You're a lawyer," Parker cried. "You know I could have you in court for talk like that."

"Don't worry," said Drew. "Before this affair is ended you'll have me in court—or I'll have you!"

They faced each other, evidently on the verge of blows. But over Drew's shoulder, Doctor Parker caught a look from the eyes of Carlotta Drew and, backing away, he stepped to the window. I turned to Mary Will. She seemed to have heard nothing; her gaze had never left the head of the stairs.

"Mary Will—what is it—what's the matter?" I said softly.

"Oh, go away—please go away!" she whispered. "They mustn't see us talking together now!"

Without question I did as she asked. But I was filled with amazement. How was Mary Will involved in the murder of Henry Drew?

CHAPTER VI

While Detective Barnes was upstairs, fifteen or twenty minutes passed, duly recorded by the busy clock in the hall. Gloomy with foreboding, I sat staring at a Chinese print on the wall. It was a cheery little thing, representing an execution. I wondered about the most vitally interested party, who appeared to have completely lost his head. Was he guilty? Or had he, an innocent man, been caught up in a net of circumstantial evidence while the real culprit went free? It was for me a most interesting question.

The bald little detective was coming down the stairs. His face was very serious; he held one hand behind his back. Mary Will was staring at him, fascinated, and to my surprise he walked straight up to her.

"If you don't mind, Miss Tellfair," he said, "we will go back to your story for a moment."

"Yes," breathed Mary Will. All color vas gone from her face.

"Your room upstairs—it's the blue room to the left, on the second floor?"

"It is."

"When you went up to get the smelling-salts for Mrs. Drew, you took the time to go first to your own room, didn't you?"

"I—I did."

"You wanted to hide something?"

"Yes."

"Something you had picked up from the side of the dead man in the dining room?"

Mary Will nodded; her face was the color of that tablecloth old Drew had seized in his last moment of life.

"You don't seem to be up on this sort of thing, my girl," Barnes went on. "Under your mattress was a pretty obvious place."

He brought his hand round from behind his back, and when I saw what the hand held, I had difficulty repressing the cry that rose to my lips. For the detective held a small Chinese knife, with a handle of grape jade, carved in the shape of some heathen god. It was unique, that knife. There could hardly be another like it in the world. I had bought it from a merchant far in the interior of China, and on the boat coming over I had shown it to several people, Mary Will included.

"It was the worst thing I could have done." Mary Will was sobbing now. "But I was so excited—I had no time to think."

Out of the murk of tule-fog and hatred and murder, one dazzling thing flashed clear—and nothing else mattered. I was a happy man.

"You did that for me!" I cried. "Mary Will—you're wonderful!"

"Then this is your knife?" Barnes broke in, holding it before me.

"No question about it," said I.

"How do you account for the fact that it was found beside the dead man?"

I turned in time to catch the look that passed between Parker and Carlotta Drew, and hot anger filled my heart.

"It was stolen, of course," I said.

"Of course," smiled the detective.

"I had not missed it yet," I went on, "but it must have been taken from my luggage, in the stateroom, sometime today. There were just two men who had access to that luggage. One was the dead man, who could hardly have taken it."

"And the other?" cried Mark Drew suddenly.

"The other," said I, "was Doctor Parker, who at seven-thirty tonight claims he was lost in the fog."

"Nonsense!" said Parker. "What motive—"

"Motive enough!" cried Mark Drew angrily. "A secret love-affair with my father's wife that has been going on for more than a year. A lust for money that is famous on the China coast—along with your well-known lack of scruples in stopping at nothing to get it. Motive, my dear Doctor—"

"You think," sneered Parker, "that I would paw over this man's luggage—that I would steal his silly knife?"

"Why not? A man who would steal another's wife would hardly stop at the theft of a little weapon like this!" Drew turned to the detective. "Sergeant Barnes, this man claims that at the time the crime was committed, he was walking from his hotel to this house. There are good pavements, good sidewalks, all the way. Let me call your attention to his shoes. They are unbelievably wet; they are muddy."

"Rot!" snarled Parker. "That means nothing. The sidewalk was torn up before a new building. I couldn't see where I was going. I got rather deep into the water and mud."

"You are in rather deep, my friend," cried Drew. "I'll grant you that."

Other hot words passed between them, but I did not listen. I had turned to Mary Will.

"Whatever happens," I said, "I shan't forget what you tried to do for me."

"Oh—it was all wrong," she whispered. "I see that now. I have harmed you dreadfully—and I only meant to help. I did it on the spur of the moment. Why I did it I can't imagine."

"Can't you? I can. Your first instinct was to protect the man you love."

"No—no," she protested.

"Poor Mary Will. All your denials won't avail now. The deed is done. You supposed that I had lost my head and killed Henry Drew."

"It was silly of me—I didn't stop to think. And everything looked against you—I saw you running out of the window."

"Everything is still against me. Are you, Mary Will? Look at me." She raised her eyes to mine. "Mary Will—I did not kill Drew. You believe that, don't you?"

"I believe it," she answered. "Nothing will ever make me change."

"That's all I wanted to know," I cried.

All my depression, all my gloom was gone, and it was in almost a gay mood that I turned to face the detective. He had waved aside Mark Drew's insinuations against Parker and was standing before me.

"Mr. Winthrop," he said, "you had quarreled with the dead man. You claim that he and his partner, Doctor Su, had defrauded you. You admit all that. You admit that this is your knife which your sweetheart—this young woman—found by the body."

"Yes," I replied, "that's all true. I admit also that things look rather badly for me. But in spite of all you have discovered, I did not kill Henry Drew. As you go further into the matter you must find that out yourself. Surely there must be some other evidence—I don't know what it can be. Perhaps when you have talked with Doctor Su Yen Hun, he can throw some light—"

The door opened and Riley came into the room. His great red face proclaimed him the bearer of news.

"Sergeant," he cried, "I went to Doctor Su's house, as ye told me to—"

"Yes, Riley."

"The place was dark. I rung the bell four times—mebbe five—nobody answered. I knew it was important, so I went round to the back. The kitchen door was open—"

"Go on."

"I went inside. Sergeant—there wasn't a livin' thing in the house. Not one. But he was there. Doctor Su Yen Hun, I mean. He was layin' dead in the middle of the library floor. Somebody'd got to him an' stuck a knife between his ribs!"

My heart seemed to stop beating. A moment of dreadful silence fell.

"Did you examine the wound?" Barnes inquired.

"I did," said Riley, proud of himself. "An' it was exactly like the one poor Mr. Drew got. Yes, Sergeant—if you ask me, the same hand done for 'em both. I waited till Detective Curry arrived, an' then—"

"Yes, Riley. Thanks. You'd better go back to your beat." As Riley went out Barnes turned to me. "This was Drew's partner in the Yunnan mine," he said. "The other man you say had cheated you?"

I tried to speak but the words would not come.

"Mr. Winthrop," the detective went on. "I'm sorry, but I have no other course—"

"Wait a minute." It was Mark Drew who spoke. "I beg your pardon, Sergeant. You are conducting this case, I know, but naturally my interest is keen. I tell you flatly I do not believe this young man is guilty of my father's murder."

"Thank you, Mr. Drew," I said.

"It's an old saying and a true one," Barnes remarked, "that there's a motive behind every killing. Find that motive and you've got your man. The motive in this case is clear: revenge."

"But there's another one of us who may have had a motive," said Drew. His eyes were on Parker.

"I can't arrest a man because his shoes are muddy," replied Barnes peevishly. "You know that. No, everything points to this young fellow. He had the motive. His story of his actions after the crime is ridiculous. His knife was found—"

"But before you arrest him," pleaded Drew, "there are so many matters still unaccounted for!"

The voice of Barnes was very cool and unfriendly.

"I recognize your interest," he said. "If there is any clue I have not considered—any matter you think I should investigate further—"

Mrs. MacShane came into the room, bearing a tray of steaming coffee cups. She placed her burden on a table.

"I—I hardly know," stammered Drew. "I'm not criticizing you, Sergeant, but...there are the fifty candles. Yes—by heaven—the fifty candles! There's mystery in them. Whose birthday is this?"

Mrs. MacShane suddenly lifted her head and came over into the center of the group.

"I know whose birthday it is," she said.

"You know?" cried Drew. "Then in heaven's name, tell us!"

"Your father explained it to me tonight," the old woman went on. "He come into my kitchen with the fifty little pink candles in his hands, an' he asked me to put them on the cake. 'If I may make so bold, sir,' I says to him, 'whose birthday is it today?' An' he says to me, 'It's the Chinaman's,' he says. 'It's Hung Chin-chung's.'"

"The Chinaman's!" Mark Drew cried.

"But why should my husband give a birthday party for Hung Chin-chung?" asked Carlotta Drew, amazed.

"Just what I asks myself, ma'am," Mrs. MacShane went on, "but Mr. Drew didn't tell me. He just repeated that it was Hung's birthday. 'Yes, Mrs. MacShane,' he says to me, 'Hung was born fifty years ago today in a little house near some queen's yard in Honolulu—out on that beach—what is it now, the one there's all the songs about? Oh, to be sure! 'out on the beach at Waikiki.'"

CHAPTER VII

The beach at Waikiki! Mrs. MacShane's unexpected bit of evidence had a fantastic ring. I had never been to Honolulu, but instantly I heard the tinkle of ukeleles, the murmur of breakers pouring in over a coral reef. I saw coconut palms outlined against a vivid sky, the brown boys riding in, erect and slender, on their surf-boards. By what stretch of the imagination could all this be connected with the murder of Henry Drew?

I looked about that strange little group gathered in the gloomy room of the house on Nob Hill. Evidently they were all asking themselves the same question. Carlotta Drew and Doctor Parker exchanged a glance of surprise. In Mary Will's eyes, I saw the light of romantic memory; stopping off on her way to China, she had known Waikiki Beach in the moonlight when the Southern Cross hung low. Detective Barnes stood blinking at Mrs. MacShane with what was, for him, a rather stupid expression. Suddenly Mark Drew leaped to his feet and began excitedly to pace the floor. Barnes turned toward him.

"Well, Mr. Drew—and where does this get us?" he inquired.

"I don't know," said Drew. "But it may get us quite a distance before we're finished."

"I can't follow you," the detective replied. "Though it is a rather startling bit of news, I'll admit that. The birthday of Hung Chin-chung! Born fifty years ago in Honolulu. Your father thinks so much of him he decides to give him a birthday party. He goes to a lot of trouble to get candles, and—say, how long was the Chinaman with your family?"

"Twenty years," said Mark Drew.

"That explains it," Barnes replied. "Twenty years! If we could keep a servant twenty years, we wouldn't stop at a birthday party. We'd give him a deed to our house and lot. Well,

Mr. Drew gives the Chinaman a party; an eccentric thing to do, but then, he always was—er—different. And what of it? We can't argue that Hung picked this occasion to kill his master. Unless he was dissatisfied with the thickness of the frosting on the cake or peeved because Mr. Drew made a mistake about his age." The hour was late, and Sergeant Barnes seemed a bit peeved himself. He turned again to me. "No," he said firmly, "it all comes back to this young man. He had a grievance not only against Henry Drew, but against the other murdered man, Doctor Su Yen Hun. His knife has been found. He was caught running away in the fog."

Mary Will was on her feet facing the detective, her eyes flashing, her cheeks aflame.

"How dare you!" she cried. "How dare you insinuate that Mr. Winthrop is capable of killing a man! You should know better."

"How should I?" asked Barnes.

"Why—just by looking at him," said Mary Will.

Barnes smiled.

"My dear young lady, I'm mighty sorry for you," he said, "but all the evidence—"

"Once more," put in Mark Drew, "I'm going to ask you to wait."

Barnes said nothing, but turned and stared at him with annoyance plainly written on his face. Mary Will sat down again, and I gave her hand a grateful squeeze. Mark Drew went over to his father's wife.

"As you know," he said, "I have been out of touch with my family for the past five years. During that time what should you say was the nature of the relations between Hung and my father? Were they as friendly as ever?"

Carlotta Drew stared at him coldly. She had not forgotten his recent snub of her; she never would.

"Your father and Hung were master and servant," she said. "That's all I know. I made no effort to pry into your father's private affairs. I felt that the details would be too—unsavory."

"Mr. Winthrop?" Drew turned to me "You said a while ago that there were only two men who bad access to your luggage in the stateroom of the China boat—my father and Doctor Parker. On second thought—wasn't there one other?"

"Yes," I nodded. "It had not occurred to me before, but Chin-chung was frequently there. He spent the morning there today, packing your father's bags."

"Nonsense!" said Detective Barnes decisively. "This birthday party is a false lead. If it means anything at all, it means that Mr. Drew was fond of the Chinaman. And it must mean, too, that the Chinaman was fond of the old man."

"Fond of him?" repeated Mark Drew. "He ought to be, that's sure. My father saved his life!"

The detective stared at Mark Drew in surprise.

"Saved his life? When? Where?"

"Twenty years ago in Honolulu. Let's see—this is the fifth of December…yes, of course, twenty years ago to a day!"

Barnes sank wearily into a chair.

"Well, if you can make it short and snappy—I suppose I ought to hear about it," he said. "Though if the old man saved Hung's life, it doesn't stand to reason that the Chinaman would—oh, well, go ahead."

Mark Drew leaned against a table and folded his arms.

"I'll try to be brief," he began. "As I say, it happened twenty years ago, in December, 1898. I was a kid of twelve then. I'd gone to the Islands with my father aboard his bark, the *Edna-May*; he owned a fleet of sailing vessels that made Honolulu from this port. Every detail of that trip stands out in my memory, clear-cut to this day. And no wonder, for I was an imaginative boy, a great reader, and I was standing for the first time on the threshold of the South Seas.

"The day of which I speak was to be our last in port. Late in the morning my father invited me to go ashore with him for lunch. We went from the dock to King Street, and I was all eyes, drinking in Honolulu for the last time. Even in those days it was the melting-pot of the Pacific; a dozen races mingled on the pavement. But you don't want a description of the town. However, the picture returns and thrills me even now. We turned off King Street, into Fort. In front of a building that housed the United States District Court, we met a man named Harry Childs coming out. Childs was a lawyer out there, somewhat shady I imagine, but useful to my father, who traveled much in the shade himself—I make no secret of it. Childs carried a few law books under his arm, as I recall, and he looked warm and depressed and rather sullen.

"'Well, Harry,' my father said, 'how did your case come out?'

"'Lost it, of course,' said Childs. 'That man Smith has it in for me. Oh, well, it's all in the day's work. But I'm sorry for poor Chang See. Shipped back to China—they'll put him on the *Nile* tonight. It's his death sentence, Mr. Drew!'

"'Too bad,' my father said. 'As I told you, I could have used him. Hung Chin-chung died on the way over—there's all his clothes waiting for someone to wear them—and his name too. I could have landed your man in San Francisco with no trouble at all. Too bad.'

"Childs looked at my father in a queer way.

"'When are you sailing?' he asked.

"'About six,' my father said.

"'The *Nile* sails for China about dusk,' Childs said. 'If I were you I'd wait until it goes out. I'd wait—about an hour—or as long as may be necessary.'

"'I'll do that, Harry,' said my father. He smiled.

"'You might have a visitor,' Childs said and went on his way down the hot street. My father and I went to the Royal Hawaiian Hotel and had lunch.

"Of course, at the time I had no idea what this conversation between Childs and my father meant. I remember standing that evening at the rail of the *Edna May* just before we sailed. The quick tropic dusk had fallen; Tantalus and Punch Bowl Hill were blotted out. From the row of shacks along the water-front came yellow light and laughter and the voices of men singing. My father happened along and ordered me to bed. He was robbing me of those last precious moments in port, and I resented it, but I dared not disobey. I went to his cabin and climbed to the upper berth, which was mine. In about half an hour the *Edna May* got under way. My wonderful journey was entering its final stage—"

"Please," broke in Detective Barnes, glancing at his watch.

"I know," said Mark Drew, smiling. "I'll hurry on. Pretty soon my father came to the cabin, sat down at his table and began to look over some papers. I dozed off—and woke up with a start. A lean, solemn Chinaman was standing just inside the cabin door. It was my first sight of the man whose birthday my father was celebrating here tonight.

"'You are Chang See,' said my father, 'and the *Nile* sailed without you.'"

"The Chinaman bowed, and something resembling a smile flitted across his impassive face.

"'I see you've got dry things,' my father went on. 'Hung's clothes suit you all right, eh?' Again the Chinaman bowed. 'Well—listen to me,' said my father. 'I have called you Chang See for the last time. From now on you are Hung Chin-chung , the same servant I took with me when I left the Gate.'

"'I understand,' said Hung—I may as well call him that, for I have never known him by any other name. He spoke good English, even then. 'You have saved my worthless life,' he went on and drifted off into a flowery sentence intended as an expression of gratitude. My father cut him short.

"'Yes,' he said, 'I've saved your life. And I expect something in return.' Of course he did. I was only twelve, but I knew he would, even then.

"'Anything you ask—' began the Chinaman.

"'I want a confidential servant—one I can trust absolutely,' my father told him. 'A man who will stick by me day and night, make my interests his, guard my safety. There are certain matters…my life has been threatened. Lie down, Mark, and go to sleep!' he added sharply, for I was leaning over the side of my bunk, wide-eyed. 'I've given you your life,' he finished to the Chinaman. 'Now I ask that you devote it to me.'

"Hung—or whatever his name was—thought for a moment. To his Oriental mind a promise was a promise and not to be lightly given, even under such extraordinary circumstances. I am trying to be brief, Sergeant Barnes. I'll sum up the discussion that followed in a few words. Hung was willing to serve my father—but for how long? He said something about returning to China to spend his last days there. There should be a limit, he thought. After a time they set it at twenty years. This was the fifth of December, the anniversary of Hung's birth at Waikiki thirty years before.

From that moment on to his fiftieth birthday, he agreed to do as my father wished.

"I was once again pretending to be asleep. My father came over and shook me. 'Wake up, Mark,' he said. 'This is Hung Chin-chung. He has agreed to act as my servant for the next twenty years, if we both live that long. My friends will be his friends, my enemies his enemies; he will guard my life as his own, and every request I make of him, no matter how trivial, he will comply with. Is that right, Hung?'"

"Hung promised on his honor and the sacred honor of his ancestors."

"'When he reaches his fiftieth birthday, I will release him from his promise,' my father said. 'You are a witness, Mark.

Don't forget.' He turned to the Chinaman. 'Now, go to your bunk. I'll have a talk with you in the morning.'

"How well Hung kept his word I know probably best of all. He became my father's shadow. Into what unsavory paths his devotion led him, I don't know. My father's activities were many—there was talk of the opium trade in those days. No doubt Hung was a useful go-between. Twice he saved my father's life when it was attempted by revengeful members of Hung's own race.

"Today, on his fiftieth birthday, as you can see, his long period of slavery—there is no other word—was ended. I know my father had grown very fond of Hung, and there was in his nature an odd sentimental streak that no doubt led him to hit on the birthday party as a fitting climax to all those years of devotion. Probably it was not so much to honor Hung that he lit the fifty candles on the cake; he wanted to call the attention of the world to the remarkable loyalty that he had inspired and, in honoring Hung, honor himself." Mark Drew paused. "That's all, Sergeant. I'm afraid I haven't helped you much, at that."

"Very interesting, Mr. Drew," said the detective. "But it gets us nowhere—nowhere at all. It establishes beyond question that Hung was under an obligation to your father, that he was always very devoted to him—"

"Yes," said Mark Drew sharply. "But you forget that the obligation has been paid. Today Hung was released from his promise—he was a free man again. What has been going on in his mind these twenty years? You and I don't know—we can't know. What white man could?"

"You mean to say," Doctor Parker put in, with what seemed to me a quite hopeful look in his eyes, "that you think Hung's first act as a free man was to murder his benefactor?"

"There's a bare chance of it," Drew replied. He turned again to the detective. "After all, there is a very thin line dividing gratitude and hate. If you saved my life tonight I should be grateful. Tomorrow, next week, possibly next year, I should still be grateful. But after twenty years—if you had reminded me of it every day—isn't it quite likely—"

A door at the rear of the room opened suddenly and Hung Chin-chung came in. Noiselessly, on his padded slippers, he crossed the polished floor to the long table on which Mrs. Mac-Shane had put the coffee. His yellow face might have been hidden behind the curtain of a tule-fog for all the expression one could read there. He gathered up the stray coffee cups and piled them on the tray.

No one moved or spoke. Deliberately Hung lifted the tray to his shoulder, swung on his heel, and strode to the door through which he had entered.

"Hung!" said Barnes sharply.

Hung paused, turned so we could see his face, and waited.

"This was your birthday, eh, Hung?" said Barnes.

"Yes."

"The fifty candles—the cake—all for you?"

"Yes."

"Mr. Drew was very fond of you. Why?"

"Why not?"

"Answer my question!" The detective reddened with anger.

"I have served Mr. Drew with honor for many years," said Hung.

"And you were about to leave his service. Where are you going? What are your plans?"

"I return to China."

"On what boat?"

"I have not yet decided. That is all? Thank you—"

"Wait a minute! Tell me—you were very fond of Mr. Drew?"

"Why not?" Hung's hand was pushing open the door.

"I want an answer!" shouted Barnes.

"For one word," said Hung, "a man may be adjudged wise. And for one word he may be adjudged foolish. I have spoken enough."

"Hold on there!" Barnes cried, for Hung was going out.

"Let him go," said Mark Drew quickly, and the Chinaman disappeared.

Barnes threw up his hands.

"All right—if you're handling the case," he said angrily.

"I should like to, for a few moments," said Drew, smiling. "Where the mind of an Oriental is concerned, one man's efforts are as good as another's."

"I was on the Chinatown squad ten years," Barnes retorted. "But if you know more than I do—"

"I know more about Hung, perhaps. Mrs. MacShane—go to the kitchen. If Hung starts to come upstairs by the back way, let Sergeant Barnes know at once. He will pass the word on to me. Now, Sergeant, if you will lend me that flashlight you had in the garden—"

With surprising meekness Barnes handed it over.

"What are you going to do?" he asked.

"Explore," smiled Drew. "We all have our pet theories. Yours inclines to this young man." He nodded toward me. "Mine, up to the time I understood the matter of the candles, favored our friend, Doctor Parker. I'm sorry to say I believe I was mistaken. I'm going up to find out."

"Hold on," said Barnes. "During those twenty years Hung served your father, do you know of anything that occurred... anything that might account for what happened here tonight?"

"A fair question," Drew said. "I'll answer it when I've had a look about Hung's room."

He went quickly up the stairs, and again silence fell in that cold and musty room. Mary Will moved closer to me on the sofa. Doctor Parker rose and lighted a cigarette, then with an air of assumed carelessness drifted to the side of Carlotta Drew, who sat near the stairs. They talked eagerly in low tones; evidently they had much that was important to say to each other. Ignoring us all, Barnes sat staring gloomily into space. He seemed for the moment a discouraged man.

The telephone, which was in a closet under the stairs, rang sharply. Barnes jumped up and entered the closet, shutting the door behind him. We could hear his voice, faint, far away.

"Hello, Riley!... Yes. What is it?... Yes.... That's good.... Fine work, Riley.... Better take her to the station. Wait a minute—bring her up here first. Yes. Good-bye."

When Barnes emerged from the closet, his face was beaming. He said nothing, but ran up the stairs two at a time.

CHAPTER VIII

Mary Will put her hand on my arm. "What now?" she asked, wide-eyed.

"I wonder—"

"I'm so worried. That horrid detective still suspects you."

"Nonsense! He can't entangle an innocent man."

"Yes, he can," said Mary Will seriously. "And he will, too, unless he finds the guilty one at once."

"Then let's hope he does. But who *is* the guilty man? My choice is Doctor Parker."

Mary Will's forehead wrinkled in deep thought.

"No," she said. "I don't believe it was Parker."

"Then why did he try so hard to put the thing on me?"

"For the same reason Carlotta Drew tried to put it on you. They both honestly believe you did it."

"Mary Will—you talk like an oracle. How do you know all this?"

"Oh—I just know it. When Mrs. Drew and I were upstairs and we heard the scream, I'm sure she suspected Doctor Parker. But the minute he reached the house, with you and the policeman, he took her aside and assured her he was innocent. I was watching them and I saw the look of relief on her face."

"Well," I said helplessly, "I'm all at sea. If Parker didn't do it—"

"Then Hung did," said Mary Will firmly. "Can't you see that?"

"Hung? Nonsense! Why, there's not a shred of evidence against him. He was in his room. Much more reason to suspect me. Oh, I certainly got tangled in a pretty mess when I came up here tonight."

"I meant to speak about that. You disobeyed me. I told you on the boat—"

"Tut, tut! Maidenly reserve, and all that sort of thing. I'm mighty glad I didn't pay any attention to it. Because, however it ends, this evening has taught me one wonderful thing. You love me."

"I haven't said so."

"You don't need to. Your actions have proved it."

"Don't be too sure. Maybe I pitied you. Have you thought of that? And pity—pity isn't love."

I have said that Mary Will could be annoying at times. Loving her, I perceived, would never grow monotonous.

"If I hear any more about pity," I said fiercely, "I'll kiss you."

"Then you won't hear any more about it," she answered quickly...and added, very softly, "Not just now."

At that instant we heard Mark Drew and the detective coming down the stairs.

Doctor Parker rose and walked to the table; when they came into view he was lighting another cigarette. Sergeant Barnes carried a little bundle of something or other, which he placed beneath the cushion of a chair. Then he walked solemnly up to where I sat.

"Well, my boy," he said, "I'm going to arrest you for the murder of Henry Drew!"

Mary Will gave a little cry, and her hot hand grasped mine. I was stunned.

"This—this is ridiculous," I stammered.

Mark Drew came up and stood by the side of Barnes.

"The sergeant is a bit crude in his methods," he remarked. "What he should have said was that, with your permission, he is about to place you under arrest as an experiment. You'll understand later. Do you mind?"

"I—can't say I fancy it . . ."

"It was my suggestion," said Mark Drew.

"Oh, well—in that case," I agreed, somewhat less alarmed.

"Call Mrs. MacShane and Hung from the kitchen," said Barnes. "Get Murphy in from the back and Myers from the front." Mark Drew began to carry out these orders. "Now, my boy, if you'll let me put these on you—"

He held out a pair of handcuffs which glittered wickedly in the dim light. I saw that Mary Will was very pale and frightened, and I wasn't feeling any too cheery myself. But I held out my hands. The lock clicked shut on my wrists just as Hung came in from the kitchen, and I thought that he stared at me with unusual interest.

"My investigation is at an end," said Barnes loudly. "You are free to go, you people. You'll all be wanted as witnesses, of course."

Mrs. MacShane went slowly up the stairs. Doctor Parker had found his overcoat and was putting it on. Hung stepped forward to assist him when Mark Drew spoke.

"All right, Hung," he said. "Go to your room. I'll wait here to look after things. You've passed your fiftieth birthday—I've not forgotten—you are your own master now. Good night, and good luck!"

For a long moment Hung looked at him. Then he bowed.

"Thank you," he said. "Good night."

He went silently up the broad stairs. Mark Drew waited about two minutes, then followed just as silently. I could see him stop in the shadows at the top and stand there as though on guard. Barnes turned to the two patrolmen.

"Come on," he whispered hoarsely. "Quick! Don't make a sound. Come with me." He led them into the dining room while we waited, completely at sea. In a moment he returned to the hall, where he stamped noisily about for a few moments. He opened and shut the outer door several times.

"Now follow me," he directed, still in a whisper. "We'll all go back to the drawing-room and wait."

He led the way. Mrs. Drew, Mary Will, Parker and I followed. As we entered, Barnes turned down the lights.

Thus I came back to the room I had not seen since I left it to answer Henry Drew's pitiful cry. The fire had burned low, but the dying logs still sent forth a warm red glow. Again they were staring down on me, those stern Drews on the wall. I was acutely conscious of the handcuffs on my wrists.

We waited. From where I sat I could see that the yellow fog from the tule-fields no longer pressed against the window panes. By straining my eyes, I fancied I could make out the dim outlines of an apartment house across the street. Was the tule-fog lifting?

The glint of firelight on my pretty bracelets must have caught the eye of Barnes, for he came over and, grinning, set me free.

"Thanks," I said gratefully.

"Temporarily, at any rate," he spoiled it all by adding.

He returned to his seat. Mark Drew came down the stairs and entered the room on tiptoe. He, too, found a chair. Our wait seemed endless.

"I don't think much of your scheme, Drew," growled the detective at last. "Silly play-acting, if you ask me."

He was interrupted by the sound of heavy footsteps in the dining room. In another moment, in the big door of the drawing-room, Myers and Murphy appeared. Between them stood Hung Chin-chung.

"You win, Drew!" Barnes cried. He leaped to his feet and turned up the lights, brisk, alive, delighted. "Hello, Hung—glad to see you," he chortled.

"He was makin' his getaway by a rope from his window," Myers explained. "We grabbed him the minute he landed."

"Sure, sure," said Barnes. "Well, Hung—that's the second time tonight the old fire-escape proved a handy invention, eh?"

Hung did not speak. He faced the detective with a dignity that was somehow pathetic and hopeless.

"Don't try that stony-stare stuff on me," Barnes warned. "I know you came down that way before. I—that is, we—I mean Mr. Drew here and I—found a few strands of the rope caught in the rough ledge of the window sill." He passed round Hung into the hall, and returned with the bundle he had hidden beneath the cushion of a chair. As he now unrolled it I perceived that it was a pair of Hung's trousers, wrapped about a pair of cheap American-made shoes. "You're getting awful careless where you put your clothes, ain't you, Hung?"

The Chinaman shrugged his shoulders. "You are searching the lake for the moon," he said scornfully.

"Maybe we are," answered Barnes. "And maybe we'll find it too. Maybe the moon's dropped down from heaven—by way of a rope fire-escape." He went close to the impassive face of the Chinaman. "I've got you tagged, son, from the minute you left here to go to your room just before dinner. Wanted to charge your clothes, eh? To bring honor to your master and your master's house? Was that the reason? I don't think so. Now listen to me—and correct me if I'm wrong: You went to your room. You put on these white man's shoes in place of those velvet slippers. You took the knife you'd snitched from Mr. Winthrop's luggage when you were in the stateroom packing Henry Drew's bags. You let out the rope of the fire-escape and dropped down into the fog. It wasn't two minutes to Doctor Su's place by the back way.

"He was alone there. Did you fix that? You put the knife in him. When you came back you saw Henry Drew in the dining room. You slipped through the window and did him in, too. Before you could get back up by the rope route, Mr. Winthrop was with you in the fog—"

"I remember," I cried. "Something struck me in the face when I was close to the wall of the house. It must have been the rope."

"Sure," said Barnes. "It was. Well, Hung, you and Mr. Winthrop played hide-and-seek in the fog. When he went out into the alley, you locked the gate after him. Then you climbed to your room. You drew up the rope and put it back on the hook. You took off these shoes, all wet and muddy, and the trousers, wet and stained round the bottom from walking in the tall grass. From your window you could step out on the roof; you hid these things in a dark corner out there. But you overlooked the mud on your window-sill, the mud on the floor. You put on fresh clothes and waited for the time when you were due to meet somebody—a friend. Where were you going, you and your friend? I'll gamble there's a boat waiting for you down at the dock; faked passports, maybe none at all; a bribe here and there—money will do a lot, eh? Well, Hung, I'm sorry. I can't let you go to meet your friend. But don't worry—it's all right. Your friend will be here in a minute to meet you."

Even at that startling bit of information, Hung allowed himself no look of surprise or of distress. Again he shrugged his shoulders.

"It's all up, Hung," the detective was saying. "You haven't got a chance in the world. It's as clear as day. Your first free evening in twenty years, and you spend it killing your master and your master's best friend. Is that your idea of a pleasant night off? Now that's all from me. What have you got to say?"

"Nothing," answered Hung Chin-chung.

Mark Drew came over and stood before the Chinaman. For a long moment the beady little eyes looked straight into those of the dead man's son. Then, amazingly, they faltered, and Hung's chin fell upon his breast.

"Hung," said Drew, "I'm sorry—you must know that. But after all, Henry Drew was my father, and I was bound to find out who killed him if I could. Then, too, you had tried to involve an innocent man. I'm all at sea. I thought you were loyal to my father—I spoke of your loyalty here tonight. There can be no question of your guilt, but that does not solve the mystery for me. It only increases it. What in heaven's name was the motive behind all this?"

We heard the front door open and the sound of footsteps in the hall. Riley, huge, red-faced, triumphant, came into the drawing-room. By one arm he led an amazing little captive, a Chinese girl who seemed not more than twenty. She was beautiful in her way; at least there was something intriguing about the sleek luster of her black hair, about her crimson mouth and her figure, alluringly slender and lissom. Her face was very frightened; the dark eyes held a hunted look as they glanced hurriedly about the room—and then one of relief as they fell on Hung Chin-chung.

"Well, Riley," said Barnes, "where'd you pick this up?"

"It's as I told you over the phone," said Riley. "When I left this house to go back on my beat, the fog was lifting. I went down California. Ahead of me, standing near the corner of Grant, I see a big touring car. I hurried up to it. When he seen me coming, the driver, a snappy little Chinaman, tried to start his motor. It stalled. I come up with him.

"I thought the back seat was empty, but under a couple of blankets I finds this bit of a girl. Just as I drags her out, the car started an' the driver beat it. I thought you'd like to meet the lady."

"Delighted," said Barnes. He went close to the girl. "Who are you? What's your name?"

She shrank from him and said nothing.

"I know her," Mark Drew put in. "I was at her wedding ten years ago. She was only a child then—but there's no mistaking her. Her name is Mah-li, and she is the wife of Doctor Su Yen Hun."

"Doctor Su's wife!" cried Barnes. "Now we are getting on! A Chinese triangle—by all the yellow gods! I didn't know they had 'em. It's all up, kid," he said to the scared little figure. "Hung here has told us everything."

"That is a lie," said Hung in a voice like ice.

"Your husband's been murdered. You know that?" roared Barnes.

"I know nothing," the girl answered faintly.

"Where have you been tonight?"

"At the house of my father, Yuan-shui, on Grant Street. Since early afternoon I was there. My brother was taking me home in his car."

"Taking you home? That's a lie. Taking you to the corner to wait for somebody—somebody who was going to smuggle you on board a boat bound for the treaty ports. Come on—" The detective seized one white slender wrist. "Who were you waiting for on that corner? Who were you waiting for—tell me, and tell me the truth, or, by heaven—"

He gave her arm a brutal twist.

"Let the woman alone!" said Hung Chin-chung, and his voice sent shivers down my spine. "She was waiting for me."

"Sure, she was," said Barnes, dropping the girl's arm. "Now tell me all about it.

"To you," said Hung scornfully, "I will tell nothing." He walked up to Mark Drew. "To you—everything," he said. "Only tonight in this house you spoke of my loyalty, my devotion to your father, and my heart was heavy within me. And why? Because, but a little while before, I had slain both your father and his friend." He turned to the girl, Mah-li. "All this was to be," he explained as though to a child. "Long ago the gods arranged it. And who is man that he should struggle against the gods?" Again he faced Mark Drew. "But because you have believed in me, have trusted me, you must know that I had good and sufficient cause."

For a moment he was silent while we waited, tense with interest. In the hallway the great clock struck the hour of three.

"Ten years ago," the Chinaman continued to Drew, "I first saw this woman, Mah-li. In the doorway of her father's shop in Grant Street—the shop of Yuan-shui, merchant of curios. A girl of fourteen, slender as the bamboo is slender, dainty as the blossom of the plum, beautiful as a jewel of pure jade. I saw her there, and it came to me that the best in life was evading me—a wife and sons to worship at the graves of my ancestors."

He stepped nearer to Mark Drew.

"What you call love—that came to me. In my thoughts, the slim figure of Mah-li was always swaying gently, like a bamboo touched by the breeze. I saw myself her husband. I heard the cry of my first-born son. Yuan-shui, whom I approached, thought it could be honorably arranged. But, as you know, I was not my own master. There was my honorable promise to your father. In this room with the firelight like two torches in his evil eyes, he listened to me while I told him how Mah-li had caught up my heart and held it in her slender, perfumed hands. I asked his permission to marry. And why not? Could I not serve him as faithfully, even though Mah-li were also mine to care for? He did not speak. He was not pleased.

"Vanity! Vanity was the secret flame at which he warmed his hands, grown cold with many wicked deeds. He was vain of my loyalty to him. That cake with the candles is a symbol, a boast. Selfish, cruel, he would not share me with the woman—he must have all my time, all my care, all my devotion. He thought I did not know. He was often a fool. He called into consultation his partner in evil, Doctor Su Yen Hun, an old man from whom the years had sucked all blood, leaving him a dry, unlovely husk. Between them they arranged it. Doctor Su had no wife living in San Francisco at the time. Your father took me on a journey to the south. When we came back it was Mah-li's wedding day. She had been given to Su Yen Hun.

"Henry Drew made merry at the wedding. That night in this room I saw his triumph blazing deep in his eyes. I hated him. I hated Su, his partner. Evil men, both of them, as like in their wickedness as the twin blossoms of the pear are like in beauty. Between them they had robbed me, and I swore that the instant I was free I would kill them both. Today brought my freedom, and tonight I kept my oath."

"You waited ten years!" said Mark Drew softly.

"Why not?" said Hung. "Was I not bound by the chains of my honorable promise?"

Detective Barnes was reaching for those chill cuffs of steel that had lately been on my wrists. Hung stepped to the side of Mah-li and laid a hand on her arm.

"Do not grieve, little disappointed one," he said. "We are not to dwell together in the great house by the broad river in the village of Sun Chin. It is the decree of the gods. For you—after you have put off the white garb of your mourning—there may be another, younger husband. For me—"

"Put out your hands," growled Barnes, coming nearer.

"Once," said Hung, "in Honolulu, the city of my birth, I stood in the foreigner's court. It is a humiliation not to be endured a second time."

With a swift movement he turned his back on the detective. I alone stood between him and the fireplace, and I could see what followed.

I had last noted my knife on the table; how he got it I do not know, but now it flashed from his sleeve. The firelight glinted on the blade as, holding the handle in his two lean hands, he plunged the point toward his heart. He took one dazed uncertain step, then fell, his black hair close to the dying fire, while from her tarnished frame above, Henry Drew's first wife stared down at him. For an instant, held by this latest decree of the gods, no one moved.

Then without a sound Mah-li dropped to the dead man's side. It was Mark Drew who snatched the knife from her hand and left her there on her knees, gazing at the motionless figure on the hearth.

He was at the end of the path at last, that Chinese boy born near Queen Emma's yard, on the beach at Waikiki. Looking down at him, I was conscious of a feeling of pity—until I recalled the knife he had taken from my luggage. Then for the first time I realized all I had escaped. And quicker than the tule-fog lifting from San Francisco, all gloomy apprehension vanished from my heart.

Henry Drew's party broke up in a sort of silent awed confusion. Under the flickering gaslight in the dim old hall, Mary Will held out her hand.

"Good night," she said.

"Good morning," I answered, pointing to the clock. "Where do you imagine you're going?"

"To bed, of course."

"You could never sleep in this house. Go up and get your hat."

"Get my what!"

"Your hat. We'll come back for your luggage later in the day. Just now I propose to take you somewhere to breakfast."

"Nonsense! I can't eat breakfast with you."

"Why not?"

"It simply isn't done—that's all," argued Mary Will.

"But it will be done this time. After breakfast I'm going shopping, and you may as well come along."

"Going shopping! For what?"

"For a wife. I understand the town is filled with beautiful possibilities. And I don't want to get your hopes up too far, but I may say that I'm considering you very seriously."

"Don't be silly. It's three o'clock in the morning."

"And I love you just as I did at three yesterday afternoon. Peculiar, isn't it? Yes—I rather think I'll marry you."

"Not without looking around?"

"I'll glance the other girls over on our way to the license bureau. If I change my mind, I promise to let you know at once. Now how about the hat?"

Mary Will hesitated. The hour was not much of a help to her in her delightful stubbornness.

"I'll—I'll have to change my dress, too," she said and ran upstairs.

In the brief space of half an hour she returned. Though the fog was gone, San Francisco was still a hidden city as we walked gingerly down the steep side of Nob Hill. The sidewalk was wet and slippery. It was absolutely necessary to hold hands.

When we came out of an all-night lunch room near Union Square, dawn was breaking over the silent town. A policeman stood on a corner.

"How soon can we get a marriage license?" I asked him.

"Three hours and more," said he. "Office won't be open till nine."

"That's a long time to wait," I told him.

He smiled. "I was that way once myself."

I bought a couple of morning papers and we strolled into Union Square. There were great headlines concerning the double murder on Nob Hill. Mary Will caught a glimpse of them.

"It all seems a thousand years ago," she said. "Let's not read about it."

"Certainly not. I bought the newspapers to sit on."

I spread them over a wet bench. They served the purpose excellently. We sat close; Mary Will's lovely eyes were heavy with sleep. Gradually her head slipped down on my shoulder. The hat she had put on was small and did not interfere. It seemed the hand of Providence.

The policeman ambled by, still smiling. "She's a pretty little thing," he said softly. "Good luck to the both of you!" And he went on his way, whistling softly.

Day came. The square filled with sunshine. Busy workers hurried by—not one of them too busy for a curious glance toward our bench. Across the way, before my hotel, the bellman took up his position. He was fresh and crisp as the morning. The voices of newsboys became more insistent.

I leaned over and kissed Mary Will's warm lips.

"Wake up," I told her. "It's your wedding day."

THE WAY TO THE ISLAND

From his office in the city hall the mayor of Reed City looked out upon the glare and glitter of Main Street at midday. Signs of life were few. Beneath the awning of the Commercial House three loyal loafers stuck to their posts, mopping their wet faces with limp handkerchiefs. Skipping gingerly over the asphalt, a barefoot boy crossed the street and disappeared down a cool-looking alley. Along the rail of the courthouse park a row of horses hitched to farm wagons drooped dejectedly in the brazen heat.

But it was not the heat that engrossed the thoughts of the master politician, Conley, looking out on the town he owned from the City Hall window. At the intersection of Main and Market Streets a huge banner advised the voter to cast his ballot for "Rickert, Reform, Reed City," and it was upon this, the war cry of the "Sunday-school crowd" trying to rob him of his fourth term as mayor, that the thoughts of Conley dwelt. With shrewd gray eyes he sized up each man who appeared in the sweltering street, and unhesitatingly classified one and all, clerk, loafer, storekeeper, butcher, baker, candlestick maker, either among the boys who would be in line when he sent out the call, or among those whose loyalty to the church would lead them to vote for its smooth-voiced idol, Rickert. And the number of the latter was dangerously large.

The door of the mayor's private office swung open slowly, and a hot, uncomfortable face was thrust inside.

"What is it, Louie?" Conley asked.

Louie slipped gently inside the room and closed the door.

"A lady," he said, wide-eyed. "She wants to see you."

"What sort of a lady?" inquired the mayor of Reed City. His air was that of one acquainted with the sex's infinite variety.

"Pretty swell, I guess," answered Louie, in an awe-struck tone. "Red dress, and red shoes, and a big hat. Wants to see you on very important business."

The mayor laid down his cigar and simulated interest in the papers on his desk.

"Show her in," he commanded.

Louie withdrew. There was a rustle of skirts, a loud "Oh, in there! Thanks awfully," and a remarkably dressed woman appeared in the doorway. Conley rose and gallantly offered a chair, closing the door behind his visitor as he did so. She thanked him with a sickening smirk that was meant to be gracious. Her dress, her shoes, and her hat were as Louie had described them; there was also red paint on her cheeks that the sun had rendered shining and greasy. The red of her shoes was yellowed with dust; there was dust on the hem of her skirt.

"I've been looking for you all morning, Mr. Conley," she began, feeling cautiously of her back hair.

"Yes," answered the mayor, somewhat embarrassed. He ran his thick fingers aimlessly through the pockets of his coat. "Yes—I'm pretty busy," he explained.

"My name's Violet—Violet Day," said the woman. "You've heard of me, I guess."

"Why—er—yes—just heard, that's all," answered the mayor. "Until now I never had the pleasure of meeting you."

"I thought you'd know *of* me, anyhow," continued Violet coyly. "I go round a good deal. And I've been mighty good friends with a friend of yours, Mr. Conley. You know who I mean—Frank—Mr. Regan, I should say."

"Yes—to be sure—with Frank," agreed Conley blindly.

"He is a close friend of yours, isn't he?" the woman wanted to know. "They say he's done a lot for you—the sort of help a man in your position needs." She pressed her handkerchief to her cheek; it was red when she took it away. "He is a good friend of yours?" she insisted.

"Why, yes—I'm very fond of Frank," replied the mayor. "But now that we've been introduced—"

"I'm coming to that," the woman interrupted. "Of course you know that somebody beat poor old Judge Berkeley up last night—and that they've pinched a negro for it?"

"Certainly I know it," answered Conley. "It has caused quite a stir. A rather brutal—"

The woman leaned toward him quickly.

"What makes 'em think the negro did it?" she asked. "Are they sure?"

"Oh, they're sure enough," said Conley. His eyes wandered to the corner of Main and Market Streets; he smiled queerly. "That is, they think they're sure." He emphasized the "they"; it referred to the virtuous crowd whose motto was Reform, Rickert, and the good of Reed City. "The negro's been the Berkeleys' family coachman for several months, and yesterday the judge discharged him for drunkenness. He swore then he'd get even. Last night he loaded up on bad whisky, and a number of people heard him say he'd do for the judge the first chance he got. Oh, he's the man, I guess."

"Well, the case *is* pretty clear," said the woman. She tapped her foot on the floor, "Pretty clear—but you never can tell." Pausing, she began to trace the pattern of the faded linoleum with her parasol. "Maybe you'll think I'm crazy, the way I jump from one subject to another," she went on, "but—I guess we'll get to something pretty soon. The other day I was in a sal—a hotel, and I heard some men talking politics. The church crowd's giving you a hard fight."

The mayor ran his fingers through his gray hair, and frowned.

"A hard fight—the men said that," continued the woman. The smirk was gone from her face now; her eyes were cruel and calculating. "They said if you didn't have Frank—Mr. Regan—to get the South Side in line and keep it there, you'd have as much chance to carry Heaven as Reed City. They said he handles the dagos and negroes and all that tough bunch over there the way a boss handles a road gang. If Frank Regan told the South Side layout to vote for Rockefeller for mayor—the men said—why, the crowd would up and do it." She stopped, and again took up her tracing of the pattern on the floor. "I thought all this over—last night," she went on. "And I decided to bring what information I've got—to you." She stopped nonchalantly to brush the dust from her skirt; her lace collar parted from its moorings at the back. There ensued a struggle with unseen fastenings. "Maybe you'd be interested to know—the negro didn't do up Judge Berkeley," she said.

The mayor of Reed City swung impatiently in his chair, and slammed his fat fist on the desk.

"Well, what has all this to do with me?" he cried. "Why don't you go to the police?" He stopped. His small eyes opened widely, then almost closed. "Oh, it's just struck me now," he said, in a hard, even tone. "I'm rather slow this morning, ain't I? So it was Frank Regan that thrashed the judge, was it?"

The woman folded her handkerchief into a small square, and smoothed it repeatedly on her knee.

"Yes, Frank did it," she said, without raising her eyes. "He's had it in for Judge Berkeley for ten years—ever since the judge sent him—away—that time. He thought he saw his chance to get him now—with that negro talking more than was good for him. So Frank waited last night till the judge got—"

"I thought you were Frank's friend," interrupted Conley sharply.

"Frank told me all about it," she went on, unheeding. "And I remembered what I'd heard—about politics—you know. They say the negro'll get a year, at least," She looked fixedly out of the window, then took a sly look at the mayor from the corner of her eye. "Election Day is about five weeks off, I believe," she added.

Conley's face turned redder than its wont. He directed a vicious kick at his desk.

"You say you're Frank's friend," he cried. "You say that, and yet you come here and threaten to tell on him."

"I don't want to tell on him," returned the woman calmly. "He's been good to me. I'd miss him. But I remembered that you'd miss him, too. And a lady's got to live." She was simpering now. "A lady can't get along on nothing. She can't let such a chance go by."

"Well," said the mayor cynically. "I'm waiting."

"I don't ask much—only a hundred dollars." The woman's eyes were cold and bargaining again. "It's worth that to you—you'll spend a good many times that on the South Side. And what chance would you have to win with Frank in jail? If they find out it was him, that's where he'll go—things are too shaky just now for you to buy a jury off. Nobody knows he did it but me—I'll swear to that. A hundred dollars and all's lovely, and we're all good friends. I ain't asking much." She traced the pattern on the floor hurriedly, nervously.

"A hundred dollars and all's lovely," repeated Conley. He nodded toward the window at the rear of the office.

"And how about him—over there?" he asked.

"Who?" inquired the woman blankly.

"Why, the negro—in the jail," said the mayor. "What becomes of him?"

She laughed shrilly.

"Oh—him," she said. "Who cares about him? Nobody'll miss him—not the way they would Frank."

"They call this thing by an ugly name," the mayor reminded her.

"I wouldn't mention it if I was you," she answered sharply. "I ain't doing it for the love of the business. I need the money. I've got to have money soon. A lady—"

The door of the office opened, and a small, unlovely gentleman stood on the threshold. He wore the clothes of a sport; dirty gray spats adorned his shoes; his face was old beyond his years.

"Hello, Sam," he said. "Why—what are you doing here, Violet?"

The woman had started nervously and flushed under her paint.

"Hello, Frank," she said. "I—I just dropped in to ask Mr. Conley's advice about a small matter."

The mayor rose and folded his short arms.

"She wants to know which'll pay most—to tell on you or to keep still," he announced.

In Mr. Regan's world surprises were many, and he met them all with a leering calm. Smiling evilly, he closed the door, and climbed up on a table. His air was that of one decidedly at home.

"I might have known," he said, swinging his legs nonchalantly. "You can't trust a woman. They're out for the cash, first, last, and all the time."

Violet began to whimper.

"I hated to do it, Frank," she sniffed. "But I had to—I just had to. I need clothes—and—things. Don't blame me."

"Oh, not at all," replied Mr. Regan lightly, "Make all you can out of me. What's her price, Sam?"

"A hundred," answered the mayor. "It's not her price I object to."

Mr. Regan was as near to a start of surprise as he had ever permitted himself to go. He stared fixedly at the mayor.

"Object?" he repeated. "There's no question about your paying, is there? After all I've done for you? And all I'm going to do for you?"

"Oh, I'll pay all right," replied Conley, after a moment's silence. "But I—I hate to have her get around me like this."

"It is hard," agreed Mr. Regan "It's no cinch to give a woman money."

"I can't hand it over now." The mayor turned to Violet Day. "You'll have to come again. Suppose we say—tonight at eight."

"I'd rather it was fixed up and over with now," put in Mr. Regan.

"I would, too," answered the mayor. "But I haven't that much on me—and I never pay these things with checks. You'll come tonight all right, er—Violet?"

"Sure," said the woman. "I can wait that long. A gentleman's word is enough for me. And I hope there won't be no hard feelings. I like everybody happy and agreeable around me."

She swept out in a blaze of red, and Mr. Regan lighted an ill-smelling cigarette.

"Now, if that ain't just like a woman!" he philosophized. "All sunshine and smiles one minute, and stabbing you in the back the next. Well, her price ain't so bad."

"No," replied the mayor absently, "not so bad."

"The boys are all in line," continued the right-hand man. "They'll all come in strong at the finish. Tonight I can place that two thousand you gave me where it'll do the most good. Everything's fine and dandy."

"Frank," the mayor said, "don't take this campaign for a comic-opera farce. There's boys working on the other side who are wise—Pat Walsh and Bob McConnell and the rest—men who won't be tied down to church methods even if their candidate does wear a white necktie."

"Don't worry," advised Mr. Regan. "The crowd's on the band wagon. Trust me to keep 'em there."

"If I was up against Rickert alone," the mayor went on, "I'd go off on a fishing trip and let him defeat himself. But the men back of him are onto the game. Be careful, Frank. Don't take this thing as a joke."

"No Sunday-school scholar's going to snatch the reins of government out of our hands," Mr. Regan assured him. "Don't you worry."

"You can't be too careful," Conley persisted. "You can't go round sandbagging prominent citizens of nights. Why won't you keep out of trouble until after election?"

Mr. Regan's yellow face contorted with anger. He leaned quickly toward the mayor.

"See here," he cried. "Understand one thing right now. I do as I please of nights. Who are you to tell me how to act? Mayor of Reed City, eh? Well, who made you? I did—"

"Regan!" The mayor's voice boomed loud; for all his pudginess he towered over his henchman. "I'll have no talk like that from you!"

Frank Regan looked once in his master's eyes, and the fight went out of him on the instant. When he spoke again, it was a sort of scared whine.

"Who runs your campaigns?" he asked, pulling at his badly soiled collar. "Who chases the crooked votes up and down the alleys while you address the populace on Main Street? I'm getting tired of your dirty work, I can tell you."

"Get out of here, then," said the mayor.

"Oh, no offense," apologized Regan. "You get on my nerves, that's all. All you do is sit here and tell me this campaign ain't going to be no old ladies' picnic. I know that. I'm working. Why don't you come out and do a little hustling, too? You can't win by just sitting here and looking like Napoleon."

The mayor smiled foolishly, and glanced at a picture hung above his desk.

"Ever since you put his picture up there," went on the shrewd Mr. Regan, "I've somehow had the feeling that you think you're a little like him. Ruler of the people, and all that. It's silly, but I can't help it."

Mr. Conley twisted nervously in his chair.

"Nonsense," he said. "He was a great man, and I admire him. I've been reading a lot about him lately, and I admire him."

"I hope you've read far enough," said Mr. Regan, "to find out that they sent him to an island at the finish. There's plenty islands left. You better get out and hustle with the rest of us." "Of course," replied the mayor. "'I'll be with you. I guess you're a little worked up, Frank. You know well enough that I appreciate all you've done for me. I've always been liberal, haven't I?"

"Oh, I can't complain," returned Mr. Regan, adjusting the pin in his yellow tie. "That's all right. I got a bit excited. Seeing that woman here was something of a jar. The idea of jail always did make me weak on my pins. And I didn't think you jumped at paying up the way an old friend like you ought to."

"Maybe I was slow," Conley agreed. "But you see—I just happened to think of the fellow in the jail. It's a little hard on him."

Mr. Regan turned quickly, and surveyed the mayor with open-mouthed astonishment.

"You thought of—of him—of the negro," he gasped. "Well, I'll be—say, what's come over you?"

"It was only a passing thought," said Conley. "I don't know how it happened to come to me. It's gone now."

"Well, I should hope so," responded Mr. Regan. He lighted another cigarette, "Say, if they found out I punched the old boy, they'd lynch me sure. It's shocked 'em beyond words that anybody should beat up a pillar of the church. I hear on all sides there'll be trouble if the negro doesn't get the full extent of the law."

The mayor bit the end from a cigar, and felt for a match.

"He'll get it, all right," he said.

"They'll never get wise. We'll fix things up. Don't worry."

Mr. Regan rose to go.

"I'll drop in tonight about eight," he remarked. "Maybe I can persuade Violet to run up to Chicago for a spell on that hundred. It would make me nervous to have her round the next few weeks." He picked up his beribboned straw hat from the table.

"So long, Sam," he said.

"So long," Conley answered.

For a time after Regan's departure he sat silently contemplating the banner at the corner of Main and Market Streets. Then he called for Louie, who drew his pay under the title of secretary, and began the dictation of letters. He droned them off wearily, occasionally interrupted by the rattle of a wagon on the cobblestones of Main Street. Once he looked up and smiled, for the voice of Pa Martin, one of the faithful before the Commercial House, was raised in shrill prediction.

"It'll rain before night," Martin proclaimed.

Louie smiled, too. It had been the old man's daily prediction for more than a week.

But as the mayor walked home for supper it occurred to him that Martin's optimistic prediction was about to come true at last. There was an unusual coolness in the air; a sudden wind rustled through the trees and across the lawns, and rattled the awnings of comfortable-looking porches. Prosperous citizens hurrying up the avenue glanced hopefully at the sky. "It's coming tonight," they assured each other joyfully; Rain had become a sort of mirage in parched Reed City.

The mayor's wife was waiting for him on the veranda. She was small and tired, with a once pretty face marred by work and worry. Tonight, had he been the sort to notice such things, he would have discovered a new and shining glory in her eyes.

"Will it rain, father?" she asked. Her tone implied that it was for him to say.

"It will if it doesn't clear up," he answered, with a clumsy attempt at geniality. His was frequently the kind of wit that is greeted by a hurt silence ratter than a smile. "Is supper ready?" he inquired.

For the first time in years Mrs. Conley dared to ignore that query. She came closer to her husband, and then at last he noticed the strange light in her eyes.

"Father," she whispered, "a wonderful thing has happened. Beth has come home. To spend two months. She's come home— with her baby,"

Conley shut his teeth. Beth was his daughter, their only child, whose hostility to his methods had long ago resulted in hostility to himself. When, several years previous, the chance to marry and leave Reed City forever had come to her, she had accepted it so eagerly and happily as almost to break the heart of the little woman at Conley's side.

"That's fine, Mary," said the mayor at last. "It's a great thing for you, I know," He peered in through the screen door. "It'll seem funny to have a baby around again," he added. "It's been a long time since Beth left."

His wife did not reply. It needed no mere man to tell her that the time was long. The record of the years was in her heart.

He opened the screen door for her, and they went inside. At the foot of the hall stairs he encountered Beth. She was a sophisticated woman now, garbed after the fashion of the cities, and she seemed far more the stranger to him than she had been even in those last years she spent at home. Embarrassed, he kissed her lightly on the cheek.

"Glad to see you, Beth," he said.

"Thanks, father," she answered. She accepted his caress without emotion. Evidently the bars were still up.

Then from behind Beth came a small figure, its golden hair shining in the dusk occasioned by the clouds without—a little boy of about five, smiling, sturdy, breathless from the excitement of this "visit." Instantly Mrs. Conley was on her knees beside him, whispering in his ear. "What I told you—" the mayor heard her say. He held out his big hand clumsily.

"Hello, young fellow," he said.

The boy looked up, and laughed.

"Hello," he replied. And then, in answer to the promptings at his side: "Grandfather."

Instantly the boss of all Reed City was on his knees, holding the boy close. His arms trembled. A lump he had not known in years returned to his throat.

"I'm glad to have you here, sonny," he choked. "I'm mighty glad."

They went into the dining room, the mayor leading his grandson by the hand. There a hot, red-faced maid served them with soup. Seated in a high chair that had long ago held Beth herself, the boy smiled with a grave friendliness at Conley.

This was a new experience for the mayor. In something of a daze, he asked a question or two—even tried a ponderous jest for the amusement of his grandson. The boy talked more and more, pronouncing the longer words painfully but correctly. Once again he used the new word he had that day learned: "Grandfather." It was huge, mouth filling, elegant. He liked it.

Deep in the business of getting acquainted, the mayor heard his wife speak timidly.

"That was a terrible thing—that negro's attack on Judge Berkeley," she ventured. "And the judge is such a good man, too. They say that when he was hurt he was on his way to help some poor family he's been looking after. It seems there's no punishment too bad for that negro—father?"

The mayor started. He looked unseeing into the laughing face of the boy—and past it—

"Is there, father?" persisted his wife.

"That's up to the courts—not to me," Conley answered roughly. The boy was talking to him, but he did not hear.

After supper they all went out on the porch, and the boy climbed timidly to Conley's knee. Evidently the hostility between the mayor and his daughter was not to extend to the second generation. The big man held the little boy close, and sat gazing out upon the dusky avenue. It was a typical summer evening in Reed City. Screen doors slammed; voices were raised in laughter; off in the distance a piano began a popular air. The youth and beauty of the town strolled by, arm in arm; its affluence swept past in automobiles that seemed jovial three-eyed dragons in the twilight. People called happily to one another from the porches and lawns, and birds twittered noisily in the elms that bordered the avenue.

"Grandfather," said the boy slowly, "I like it at your house."

Conley held the boy closer still. He shut his teeth tightly and looked out at the town—his old hometown—the town that hated him, that was fighting him tooth and nail. This boy might have come home to a different grandfather. Conley wished, for a moment, that he had. But it was too late now—he must go on fighting—fighting the smug, respectable element among his own people. And he would lick them, too. Once more he would humiliate them. And he would at the same time hold the boy's love, his respect—he would explain to him, when he grew older, how without meaning to he had drifted into this war with his own kind. He would make the boy honor him for his fearlessness, his strength, his power over others.

Suddenly in the distance he heard the courthouse clock strike eight.

Conley sat for a moment, a sick feeling in his very soul. Then he put the boy down gently, and rose to his feet.

"I've got an engagement at the office, Mary," he said, and went in for his hat.

"It's going to storm pretty hard, I'm afraid," she called after him. "I was hoping you'd stay home tonight."

"Can't do it," he told her, coming out again. "This is important."

"Father," she pleaded, "you'll take an umbrella—" It was the old, old argument between them. Always she was urging umbrellas upon him, always he was scorning them, venturing forth unprotected while she fretted. Offering his old refusal, he heard a noise at the screen. The boy had gone inside. There was a prodigious struggle with the screen door, and he emerged, triumphant. He held out an umbrella.

"Here, grandfather," he said.

Conley took the umbrella in one hand, and drew the boy to him with the other. "Thanks, sonny," he said. He touched his coarse lips to the boy's silky hair. All the way down the avenue he still felt the clutch of a little hand at his coat collar.

The traditional calm that precedes a storm was being broken by the slamming shut of windows and the dragging in of porch furnishings. In front of the City Hall the mayor paused to gaze at an excited crowd that had gathered before the Commercial House, and a drop of rain splashed in his face. In his office the crimson-garbed Violet, even more tawdry in the flickering gaslight, sat waiting.

"You're late, Mr. Conley," she said, in coy rebuke. "I was here nearly an hour before time. You can bet I ain't missing you tonight."

"I'm sorry I kept you," he answered. "Do you mind if I smoke?"

"Sure not," she replied promptly. "I always like to have gentlemen enjoy themselves around me. Eat, drink, and be merry, I say, for tomorrow—"

She was interrupted by a vivid flash of lightning, followed by a deluge of rain.

"Well, now look at that," she cried. "If it ain't pouring. It'll just ruin this skirt and these shoes to go out after a rain like this."

The mayor took a wallet from his pocket.

"I've got the money, Violet," he said. "I hope you understand the terms of our—er—affair. You know—"

"Oh, sure," broke in the woman, her eager eyes on the pocket book. "I'm a lady. I guess my word's good. I'll keep my mouth shut."

Some one ran through the outer office, and plunged into the mayor's room. It was Frank Regan. His gay plumage hung limp with the rain. Water dripped from his straw hat, from beneath which his face, deathly pale and wet with sweat and rain together, looked out like some evil thing. He passed his hand once across his forehead, brushing back the matted hair. His knees were knocking together.

"Have you paid it?" he cried. "For God's sake, hurry up and pay it! Give her the hundred. What do you mean by sitting there like a statue? Think all I've done—I've been a good friend. Violet—you won't tell—swear you won't—" He paused for breath, leaning against the table for support. "Pay it," he whined. "What are you waiting for? Hand it over."

The mayor of Reed City and the woman he was bribing stared wonderingly at the limp, pitiable figure before them. The door of the outer room had opened and Louie had come in, but no one noticed him until he stood at the inner door. Then Regan jumped up and tried in vain to shut him out.

"Get out of here," he cried wildly. "You're not wanted here. This is a private affair. Get out!"

But Louie stood unmoved just inside the door.

"I'll only be a minute," he said, in apology. "There's something happened I though you'd want to know at once, Mr. Conley." He paused to wipe the rain from his face. "It's about Judge Berkeley," he went on slowly. "He—he died twenty minutes ago."

The mayor swung slowly in his chair; it creaked mournfully. Then he spoke, in a harsh, unnatural voice.

"From the beating he got last night?" he asked.

"Sure," Louie answered. "Of course. It seems he was hurt inside somewhere." He paused. "I'll just be going," he finished.

The silence following his departure was for a time unbroken, save for the lashing of the rain at the windows. Then the woman began to cry softly, keeping up a dreary accompaniment to the splashing on the panes. Regan moved nearer her.

"Well, Violet," he whined. "Things have changed. Prices have gone up, I guess. A hundred's not enough, eh? What do you say to a thousand? How does that suit you? A thousand? What do you say?"

"I don't know," moaned the woman. "I'm afraid. I never thought of this. I'm afraid."

"Brace up," cried Regan. "Think of the things a thousand will buy. He'll pay it—oh, that's all right." He looked pleadingly at the mayor, sitting silent at his desk. "He'll pay. He won't forget the things I've done. He's a good fellow—he's always been square with me. I know he'll pay—" His voice broke and died away in a scared whine. He half fell forward, grasping the mayor's arm. "See me through this," he whimpered, "for God's sake help me through it. They're over there threatening to lynch the man who did it. Stand by me. For years I've stood by you. She'll take a thousand—won't you, Violet?—that's a lot of money—I mean, it's not much to you, Conley. You'll take it, Violet?"

"I—I don't know," sobbed the woman. The tears were marking paths across the paint on her cheeks.

Regan leaned heavily on the mayor's chair.

"She'll take it," he whined.

"The man they've arrested," broke in Conley harshly. "The man in the jail—"

Regan covered his face with his hands.

"He's a negro," he shrieked. "He's a negro, with the soul of a rabbit. You don't mean you're thinking of him? Think of me! I've bought your votes for years. I've been your best friend on earth. It's me against him—your best friend against a negro. Oh, you ain't thinking of him!"

The courthouse bell rang out sharply above the roar of the rain. Regan uttered a cry, his knees gave way, he fell sobbing to the floor.

"Pay her," he screamed. "Pay her."

But the woman drew away, shivering. "I'm afraid," she droned. "I'm afraid."

The door opened, and Louie again rushed in.

"Mr. Conley—they're ringing the courthouse bell," he shouted. "Don't you hear them? They're ringing it. What are you sitting here for? Do you know what it means? They're going to lynch him. They're all crazy tonight. The street's full of men. They're wild."

"Lynch him?" repeated the mayor slowly. "Oh, no, they won't do that. You're excited, Louie—that's all. They won't do that."

"Yes, they will," cried Louie. "Frank's been telling round all day that you'd get the negro off. He said you owned the grand jury. They're crazy. They say you got two negroes off, but you'll never have a chance with this one. They say they'll lynch *you* if you show your face. The street's full of men. Look out if you don't believe it."

The mayor walked to the window and saw through the mist and the rain a great crowd gathered in front of the Commercial House. Men were coming on the run from all directions. At the corner of Main and Market Streets the banner of the reformers flapped like a great white arm in the wind. It was the reformers—the "Sunday-school crowd"—who were collecting below; their ideals and their civilization forgotten; mad beasts for the moment under the tyranny of the little man who was looking out on them from the City Hall window. Conley saw Louie emerge from the door beneath him and join the mob. He turned to Regan.

"Frank," he said calmly, "I've worked some pretty low deals. You know that—you suggested most of them. But this— this won't do. I'm sorry—it's an awful mix-up. But you've got to go."

"Go," cried Regan. "Go! What d'you mean? Pay her the money. He's a negro—"

"He's a man, I suppose," said the mayor. "Now listen to what I have to say. You have got something coming from me— two things. Twenty minutes in time and two thousand in money—the money I gave you for—for the other. Take what I'm giving you and get away if you can. The Chicago train leaves at nine—in fifteen minutes. There's another train south in twelve minutes. If I was you I'd be on one of 'em—and I wouldn't let any one see me boarding it, either. Twenty minutes and two thousand, Frank. Then I'm through with you forever."

"Through with me!" screamed Regan, ashen now. "I won't go! Get me out of this! The way's clear! It's easy! Haven't I done your dirty work for years? Now pay me the price."

Conley took hold of him by his narrow shoulders, and looked him coolly in the eyes.

"Sit here and let them do this thing?" he asked. "Is that the price you mean? It's too high, Frank. It's too high. Twenty minutes and two thousand, Frank. That's my offer. You'd better take it I can't explain it exactly, Frank, but—I'm sick of it all. And I'm not with you any longer,"

Regan drew himself up.

"You're a friend in need!" he sneered. "A fine friend in need! So this is the pay I get from you—this is my reward? You throw me down—for a negro. Well, I'll tell you something. I'm not going. I can stay and tell some tales myself—"

A few shouted orders came up from the street; there followed the noisy tread of many feet out of step. All over the town women hiding behind locked doors heard it, and screamed. A terrified, hunted negro, crouching in the corner of a narrow cell, heard it, and began a prayer to his long-forgotten God. Mr. Regan also heard it, and tears of rage and terror ran down his pale face.

The mayor glanced at his watch.

"Ten minutes to nine, Frank," he said. "You haven't, much time to waste."

Mr. Regan's mouth opened and shut several times, but he did not speak. He fell into a chair beside the table, and buried his face in his hands.

"I'm afraid," he shuddered, unconsciously repeating the woman's words. "I'm afraid. I'm sick. It's the thought of the jail. And they might lynch me. And this is the pay I get—from him."

The mayor shifted uneasily. The cry of a great crowd came from the direction of the jail. He ran to the door, past the woman in red who was now so pale beneath her rouge.

"Better hurry, Frank," he said. "Get away if you can. I owe you that, I guess. Better hurry—things are all wrong tonight—

I'm sorry—" Another cry came from the jail, and the mayor disappeared.

He ran as fast as he could, across Main Street, and through the wet park. The rain was falling very softly now. As he passed beneath the arc lights he looked pudgy and pathetic and funny all at once, waddling along on his short fat legs.

The yard of the jail was tightly packed with madmen. Mad himself at sight of them, Conley pried into them, pulled them apart, struck out wildly, and finally found himself on the steps facing the mob. They recognized him with an angry shouts.

"Go back," he cried. "You're crazy—drunk with excitement. Go back. This man didn't kill Judge Berkeley. I can prove he didn't. There's a woman named Violet Day will swear to it. You're all wrong."

He saw that the leaders wore masks and that the rain had plastered them to their faces, which looked like grinning skulls in the half-light. He drew back in sudden terror.

"He didn't do it," he cried again.

"Who did?" shouted a voice in the distance. The cry was taken up on all sides of him.

He staggered back against the door in the horrible silence that followed. They were waiting for his answer.

"I—I can't tell," he stammered. "I'll tell tomorrow. I've got to keep still tonight. Wait till tomorrow."

There followed another silence; he knew it was the turning point. They were weighing up the evidence in his favor. He saw their ranks falter; a half-hearted hope rose within him. Then there came a hoarse cry, and it changed all against him:

"Save the negro if you can. He's got a vote."

In a second the whole mob was moving, here and there, like ill-trained supes in a show. The refrain, "The negro's got a vote" was taken up and chanted, like the burden of a song. With it came rushing back all their hatred of him and his methods. A stone whizzed close to his head, and another. They came up the steps toward him, and he thought of the negro in the jail as he faced them. It was five minutes past nine; during one of the lulls in the shouting he had heard the whistle of a train.

"Go back," he shouted. "I'll tell! I'll tell! You're crazy to-night—you'll be sorry in the morning. I'll tell. He's been my best friend. You know that. You know why I don't want to tell. It was Frank—it was Regan—he did it! I don't know where he is—you can hang me in his place if you want to."

He sank down on the steps between the stone lions that guarded the jail door. For a moment the crowd was silent, then it drew back. No one questioned his word. The muttered comments died quickly; one by one the men whose hands had itched for the feel of a rope slunk off, ashamed, into the night.

When they had gone he rose from the wet stone steps and hurried back to his office. Louie was there alone; in the air there was such an odor of perfume as might linger after a lady with a very red dress.

"I met Frank on the stairs," Louie said, "going down them like mad. He said you was—he called you some pretty strong names. What did he mean? What's the matter?"

The mayor walked to the window and opened it, standing for a moment in the cool breeze that swept in with the rain.

"Those men over in the jail yard," he said, "they used to be my friends, Louie—long ago. I went to school with them once. And tonight when I was doing the first decent thing of my life—since I went into politics—when I was trying to save a negro, they said I was trying to save the negro's vote. That's what they think of me, and I've lived with them fifty years. Is it too late to make them think different, Louie? I wonder. I wonder."

"I don't understand—what's it all about?" asked Louie.

"It's pretty plain," the mayor said. "Your boss is through. He's done for himself." The wind rushed in through the window and caught the picture of Napoleon, banging it loudly against the wall. Conley nodded toward it, and smiled. "They sent him to an island—at the end," he said. "I guess as far as my job in Reed City goes—I'm on my way to the island myself." He settled his hat firmly on his head, and, reaching out, took up his umbrella—gently, as though he were taking a little boy's hand. "And the funny part of it is," he added, smiling, "I don't know as I care, Louie. I don't know as I care."

ABOUT THE AUTHOR

Earl Derr Biggers was born in 1884 in Warren, Ohio. He attended Harvard and received a B.A. in 1907. His first real job was as a humor columnist at *Traveler*, a Boston newspaper. He was also a drama critic there.

He successfully supported himself as a novelist and playwright from 1912 until his death from a heart attack in 1933. Today he is best known as the creator of detective Charlie Chan of the Honolulu police, though he published many non-mystery novels and short stories as well.